Natalee Caple launched her literary career in 1998 with her debut story collection *The Heart Is Its Own Reason*, which captured the attention of the *New York Times Book Review* and garnered high international praise. Her 1999 novel, *The Plight of the Happy People in an Ordinary World*, established her reputation as one of Canada's most talented young writers. Caple's book of poetry, *A More Tender Ocean*, was nominated for a Gerald Lampert Award in 2000. Most recently, she co-edited *The Notebooks: Interviews and New Fiction from Contemporary Writers* with Michelle Berry. Currently, Caple is the 2004–2005 Markin-Flanagan Distinguished Writers Programme Writer-in-Residence at the University of Calgary.

D1366605

Books of Merit

MACKEREL SKY

MACKEREL SKY

Natalee Caple

Thomas Allen Publishers

Toronto

Library and Archives Canada Cataloguing in Publication

Caple, Natalee, 1970–
    Mackerel sky / Natalee Caple.

ISBN 0-88762-143-0 (bound).   ISBN 0-88762-179-1 (pbk.)

I. Title.

PS8555.A5583M32 2004   C813'.54   C2004-900627-4

Editor: Patrick Crean
Cover images: Sky (front and back cover) by Tony Howell;
    Woman in car (front cover) by Kimm Saatvedt / f Stop Photography / Veer

Published by Thomas Allen Publishers,
a division of Thomas Allen & Son Limited,
145 Front Street East, Suite 209,
Toronto, Ontario M5A 1E3 Canada

www.thomas-allen.com

  **Canada Council
for the Arts**

The publisher gratefully acknowledges the support of
the Ontario Arts Council for its publishing program.

We acknowledge the support of the Canada Council for the Arts, which
last year invested $21.7 million in writing and publishing throughout Canada.

We acknowledge the Government of Ontario through the
Ontario Media Development Corporation's Ontario Book Initiative.

09 08 07 06 05   1 2 3 4 5

Printed and bound in Canada

Cette histoire est pour mes chères grandmères,
Gwyneth Probyn et Eileen Caple,
et mon ami fou, Nicholas Kazamia.

"There was a time when I thought a great deal about money. Then one day instead of going to my office I visited the aquarium. The concrete floors shone with condensation. The dank air smelled of brine. I found myself standing in front of a tank, staring at the sea horses hovering beneath the Exit sign. Their spiny white bodies looked like question marks carved out of ice, suspended in the seaweed behind the dirty glass. Coronets, as individual as fingerprints, weighed down their long faces. Tiny pectoral fins worked the water in figure-eights. A sign under the tank said that it is the male sea horse who becomes pregnant after sex. And then, in just a little while, he releases tiny, glassy replicas of his own body from a swollen pocket on his belly. I stared at one obviously pregnant steed, and I thought to myself, I don't know anything about the world. I don't know anything."

Guy lowers his arm and covers her shoulders. The blinds over the train windows are half-rolled, and the landscape sweeps past at an astonishing rate.

"How long until we reach Boston?" she mutters. Her eyes and her eyelids are red. The cotton shirt she is wearing bears a spatter stain from the neck to the waist.

"I wish I could start over," he whispers.

Wind floating through the grass around them makes an ocean of the field. Isabelle rests her cheek against her knee, so that her voice is muffled. Guy stares up at the mackerel-backed sky. Light streams through the gaps between tightly packed rows of wavy clouds covering most of the sky. Rippled shadows flow across the hill.

"It means that the weather is going to change."

"What?" He turns his head to look at her. Blue eyes blink at him behind a curtain of brown hair. She lifts her face.

"You've been staring at the sky," she says.

"It's a mackerel sky," he says.

"Don't worry, it doesn't mean that the weather will get worse—it might get better. It depends if we're seeing them at the beginning or at the end. Those are very high clouds, about eighteen thousand feet above sea level. It means that there's convection in the upper atmosphere. And there, you see." She points. "Those flat, wispy, flowing clouds that flick off the edges of the bank, those are mare's tails."

"What do those mean?"

"I don't know. I think they just get pulled away by the wind. Luke Howard is the name of the man who wrote the first textbook on clouds. I have it. It's really good. He was an amateur meteorologist and a chemist from London. London, England, not London, Ontario. He's the one who came up with all the names for cloud formations. You know, cirrus, stratus, cumulus."

"Are you nervous?" he asks.

"A little. Don't you want to talk to me?"

His shirt billows and deflates with the breeze. "Yes," he sighs. "I want to talk to you."

"So? You came back. You bought a train ticket from Boston. What color was the ticket?"

"Blue."

"And you handed the ticket to a man in a jacket. And then I agreed to meet you here. But you couldn't stop staring at the sky so I had to ask you questions, like, what did you think I would be like when we met?"

He looks at her. Her skin is flushed in that permanent way that pale young skin flushes over healthy muscle. Her straight, golden brown hair glows in the sunlight like sheets of burnished copper.

"I used to think that you would be a very beautiful girl one day. Martine wasn't pretty when she was a kid. But when she was your age, she was very beautiful."

She smiles at the mention of her mother.

"The way those blue eyes used to go black, pop, when

she got excited, her pupils exploded like this." He raises a fist and opens it into a wide palm.

"Yes, I know my mother. It's you I don't know."

He looks back at the sky. "No. I know you don't know me. Should we go down and have a drink at the restaurant? You can ask me questions while I have a beer."

"Yes. Okay. I'm very thirsty."

"I can tell."

Walking down the great hill, he holds back to watch her. Her sleeveless sundress shows off pale shoulders, hunched stiff. White and semitransparent, the dress has a yellow plaid band around the tiny waist that matches a ribbon around the hem of the skirt. Beneath the yellow hem her gait is stubborn.

"So what kind of girl do I have?" he calls out. "Do I have a religious girl?"

"You don't have me," she answers sullenly.

"I know how you're different from your mother. You're more stubborn. I used to be religious, you know. I used to believe a lot of things. Martine ruined all that for me."

Isabelle stops walking and looks back. She braces her hips with her hands. He notices her lips tightening. "I shouldn't have said that," he mutters. "Your mother was my only friend. She just seemed sad a lot of the time."

"Maybe with you." She returns to her descent. Strands of her hair, flung over her shoulder, bounce with each rough step and are held aloft briefly by the breeze.

Her lips purse as she examines the paper menu. Guy notices the waiter glance down the gap at the neck of her dress. The waiter is her age, twentyish, brunet with dusky skin beneath a smooth white shirt tucked into neat black pants. Isabelle looks up and they seem to see each other at once, being young and attractive beneath the trees. Guy feels suddenly irrelevant and awkward. He studies his daughter's pink mouth when she tilts her head and smiles at the young man. It's a bit of a shock to him how beautiful she is. He can't stop watching her. With effort, by narrowing his eyes, by holding his breath, he forces himself to see this pretty girl, shaped so much like Martine, as someone related to him, more than a young cousin, his own offspring. He struggles to conjure a plane of his own face in hers, to summon a paternal pride and lever out the lonely confusion.

"I dreamt about you last night," she says when the waiter leaves.

She has a long, delicate face beneath a round forehead. Her wide eyes are bordered with thick brown eyelashes. Icy blue irises surround perfect black pupils that stare out at him. Her lips are shaped like his. She has thin lips that twist a little when she renders a smile. That little oval in the middle of her upper lip, the little bulge of flesh below the divot, below the philtrum, what do you call that tiny projection? The *prolabium*, yes, it looks like his. He can see as she talks that her lips are not thin, they are narrow but they project softly. Her upper lip is slightly fuller than her lower lip, which is unusual, and the perfect oval where the two halves of her lip meet—she has a mouth like an infant—yes, that's what it looks like—soft and small and delicate. And her sloping cheeks flushed between twin curtains of brown silk, she gets those cheeks, the length of her face, and its thinness from him. Martine has a round face, with high cheekbones and small eyes. She has a European mouth, wide and generous over her teeth, and expressive, much too expressive.

"Why did you grimace just then? Are you very introverted or just very rude?"

"I'm sorry," he says, by which he means that he is confused because he hasn't been listening.

"You're staring at me. And I want you to listen to me."

It takes him a minute to respond. "I'm sorry. I'm sorry. I'm introverted. You're right, I'm very introverted and that's a little rude. What did you dream?" he asks finally.

"I dreamt that we met on the street." She sighs and looks back and forth between him and the young waiter. "We had arranged to meet and I took your hand while we were walking. At first you were pleased to have me holding your hand, but then you pulled away. I got angry at you and then you were gone."

He laughs shortly, but stops because she is giving him a hard stare.

"Why is that funny?"

"It's just funny. Other women have told me the same dream."

She puts her elbow on the table and leans her cheek against her hand.

"I didn't mean to dismiss you," he says. "You know I wrote you letters. Martine must have thrown them away. And I sent you money." He hears an unfamiliar wheedling tone infiltrate his voice.

"You're lying. She would never hide your letters from me."

"There, you see, you do know me a little bit. I could have written you letters. I had lots of paper."

"You're not funny."

He pauses. "That's because you're hungry."

"You said you were religious?"

"I was exaggerating."

"I invented a religion." She leans forward and lifts her feet out of her sandals to grip the front of her chair with dirty bare toes. She hugs her knees and smiles. "Well, I guess it's more like a myth. In the beginning," she starts.

Guy takes a breath. The blood rushes back to his brain with the relief he feels to see her smile and look at him directly.

"God created the world. He made it to be a model of the way that he felt himself in time. And then he made a man. He made him as a toy and he made him as an exact replica, a sort of doll, of God. But when he looked at the man he suddenly saw all of his own flaws the way that you can see them in another creature but not in yourself. God got so angry that he ripped out one of the man's ribs and started hitting him. The poor man, with his arms held up, and a hole in his side, just cried, 'Don't, don't.' So God stared at the man until he decided to try and make something better. He started all over and he made a woman. He always meant to go back and finish the man off. But once the woman was done and he knew he had finally made something good, he felt sorry for himself. He couldn't kill off the man, out of vanity. But he gave up the ability to make human beings to the woman because he had discovered that he couldn't trust himself."

She laughs out loud at his expression, covers her mouth with her hands and throws back her head to laugh some more.

"I have a clever girl. How unfortunate," he grumbles.

"Don't worry about it." She sighs. Her eyes look suddenly swollen. "It's all right; I'm not really clever. I just read a lot because I have a lot of time on my hands."

"That makes you mine," he mutters.

The waiter arrives. A green bottle and a clean glass are placed in front of Guy, who can barely remember ordering. A loaf of bread in a basket and a small white plate holding pools of olive oil and balsamic vinegar are placed on the table between them. Isabelle nods at the waiter and releases her knees. Her long legs fall carelessly back below the table. She picks a piece of bread out of the basket, tears it into small pieces and feeds herself between sentences.

"When you called and said you were coming to Ravel, I asked Mom about you."

He nods, and squeezes the beer bottle absently. "What did she tell you?"

"I asked her if she would be upset if I came to meet you, and she said no. I think she expected you to call one day."

"She's been expecting that for a long time."

"Twenty years. I don't think she would have cared if you didn't call. She never said very much about you, except that you grew up together. Of course I know about my grandparents. That your father and her father used to import and export illegal items across the American border together."

He raises his eyebrows but says nothing.

"I know that my grandfathers were mean, until they left. And then my mother and my grandmother helped you and your mother get on your feet. Mom babysat you a lot. You were sixteen when you finally slept together, and she was twenty-five. She wanted me, and she said that she chose you for my father because she knew you would get scared and leave."

"That's an interesting summary of our family history. I don't like the way that I come across. How could she know what I would do?"

"You were sixteen," she says gently. "When I was sixteen I would have run away too. Don't worry, I don't blame you. Sally and Mom took excellent care of me. I don't even know what a father is for. I don't mean that I'm not glad to see you. I'm curious about what happened to you. I feel sorry for you. Like you were a friend of mine."

"That's very generous." He clears his throat and crosses his legs, knocking the metal tabletop with his knee and tipping his beer, which sloshes out of the glass. "Shit! Sorry. I didn't mean to say that." He sweeps the spill off the table with the side of his hand, splashing froth on his trousers and shoes. Isabelle watches him quietly as he fusses with his trousers, dabbing at the beer stain with a paper napkin.

"Do you want to stay with us?" she asks at last.

"No. I have a room booked in Estérel," he says. "I'm only staying a few nights. Then I'm going back to Boston."

She nods. "There's nothing but our house in Ravel now. They burned down your old house when I was just a kid."

He pictures the two houses at the end of the long, lonely road out of Estérel. He balls up the damp napkin and releases it on the table. "Who burned down my house?"

She shrugs, and for a moment he feels sorry that he asked about his old house, his old stupid house where they lived with his father. What does it matter whether it stands or not? "I don't care. I don't care about that house," he says.

"I think the police took it apart after your father was arrested. I think he was arrested."

Guy shakes his head. He doesn't know. "I haven't seen him since I was a kid."

"And then the police came and because the house was abandoned they searched everywhere, the walls and floors, to see if it had been used as a storage space. When they didn't find anything, they left. Of course, because there were no men in our house they left us alone. We hadn't had any contact with my grandfathers since Mom and you were kids. And then the poor old house was left behind all ripped apart with no one to protect it. So someone burned it down. Maybe kids. Maybe someone who knew your dad. Maybe the police themselves."

"Poor old house," Guy agrees. "I want you to know," he starts.

"Speak up, I can't hear you."

The very table seems to lower with his sigh. "I know you know about your grandfathers and I want you to know that I wasn't like them. I mean, of course I wasn't a criminal. But also I didn't, I mean I *did* leave your mother. But I want you to know that I regret leaving. I thought about coming back. I thought about you." He looks helplessly at the pretty grown woman who sits across from him. He did not think of her, he must admit. The daughter he had imagined was miraculously still a child.

"At least come for dinner. At least come and see Mom. We've barely talked. It was a long train ride for you to get here. You must want something. Something must be on your mind."

RAVEL

His hand sweats around the leather handle of the battered suitcase. The comely silvery light, so specific to summer afternoons in the Laurentians, softens everything it touches. Martine's house is as he remembers it, a small brick dwelling in a U-shaped lot, dwarfed by the sky. The house is surrounded by a spiky line of pine trees, sugar maple, basswood, oak and sumac, and framed from a distance by low Precambrian hills. It all looks unaltered, except that the climbing roses have grown to completely cover one side of the house, and the flowers that embroider the wall are yellow, and not red as he had anticipated.

"The big apple tree is gone."

"Yes. It died a few years ago. We left it for a year even though it went all black and skeletal, and then Mom cut it down."

"She cut it down herself?"

"She used a chainsaw. The tree fell on me because I was standing behind it, waiting to guide it. I didn't think it would be so difficult to catch with all the branches. I also didn't think it would be so heavy," she says wryly. "Mom had to cut it in pieces around me before I could get out from under it."

She locates a key in her purse and turns the key in the scarred lock, bumping the door with her shoulder to open it.

The hallway smells of ashes and perfume. It seems to Guy as if the banister is on the wrong wall and that the stairs curve more than they used to, or take an extra turn before they reach the top. The carpet runners seem right, a pale blue length rolling out over the dark wood floor, thin patterns of red flowers faded in the patches of sunlight that fall through the windows. A crystal chandelier hangs halfway along the ceiling in the hallway. Dust blurs the light refracted by the tears. The room directly to his right is still a library, all the walls hidden behind bookshelves.

"When did she get the chandelier?"

"I don't know," Isabelle says. "I always remember it being there."

Together they pad down the hall in bare feet. The curtains are drawn in the living room, adumbrating night in the small space cramped with furniture. Isabelle walks to the couch and crouches down. It takes a second for him to see that beneath the pile of quilts, her mother is curled, napping. Martine lifts her face to kiss Isabelle and throws a pale arm around her neck.

"Where's Harry?" he hears Isabelle whisper.

"Sulking," her mother answers. She lifts her arms over her head and stretches. The quilts fall away from her upper body. She is wearing something dark and flimsy with a loose, scooped neck. Her throat and chest glisten with sweat. Her large breasts are exaggerated by her arched posture. A wave of recognition rolls over Guy as he sees her body, echoed by a slight, involuntary engorgement, and a tender roll of his stomach. Martine reaches beneath the shade to turn on the reading lamp. The yellow light behind the messy flow of her hair, her slow smile expanding and her slanted, sleepy eyes all bring him crashing home. For a second he cannot hear her voice as she mutters, "Are you coming into the room or not?"

"I'm coming," he says. "It's good to see you, Martine. I met—her." He gestures weakly toward Isabelle. Somewhere deep in the house the telephone rings.

"I heard you were going to do that. So what are you doing here, Guy?"

"I came for dinner. Isabelle invited me."

Martine inhales through her teeth, whistling quietly as she nods. "Open a bottle of wine, Isabelle. Are we expecting anyone else?" She glances about as if to check the armoire, the curtains, the doorway for emerging figures. Isabelle leaves the room. Martine looks directly at Guy. He watches her gaze travel up from the floor over his body to his face. He shivers.

"When are you going to answer the phone?" he complains.

"I'm not going to answer it."

She stands, and as she stands he realizes that he expects her somehow to be taller than him, that he feels tiny again, in this familiar room with her.

"Well, Guy Vidoq," she says. "You look beautiful. You look like a man."

VIEUX MONTRÉAL

Jim Mann grabs a thin hotel towel from a chrome bar beside the bathroom counter. He wipes up the refuse from his shaving. A radio sings in the room behind the open bathroom door. He leans forward to examine his face in the mirror. He is an older man, but still vain enough to hold his neck and examine the line of his jaw circumspectly. He grins to check his teeth. He turns his head and folds each ear to check for wild hairs sprouting from the tops. He smooths his white hair with a black comb.

Dressing is a matter of transformation. His thin, pale legs disappear into crisp navy pants. His protruding breastbone is buttoned beneath a pale pink shirt. He clips French cuffs at his narrow wrists with a pair of small, subdued mother-of-pearl cuff links. On his left wrist he buckles a plain Cartier watch with a white face. Thin as a dime, the glass face gleams between the bands of a black leather strap.

Expertly he loops and knots a mauve silk tie under the collar around his sagging throat. He draws on a double-breasted high-gorge navy jacket and fondles one of its six buttons between manicured fingertips. With the jacket closed, his tie puffs out discreetly over the shallow V of shirtfront. He fusses with his pocket square—purple silk and bearing rococo scrolls, it resists his effort to achieve a balance of controlled fold and delicate disarray. He pauses as he hears a door open and the tinkling sound of someone dropping a set of keys on the rickety card table beside the wooden coat rack in the bedroom.

"Jules?" he calls calmly, barely raising his voice above speaking level. He listens briefly for an answer and then resumes his grooming. He dots spicy, leather-scented cologne behind his ears, Hermès, Rocabar. Glancing at his cuffs, he tsks loudly. A tiny constellation of brown spatters mars the edge of one cuff. He shakes his head and begins undressing.

"Suceux de balus. Jules, where are my other shirts?" he calls.

A voice responds from beyond the door but he cannot interpret the answer.

"Dans le bain?" He sounds incredulous. In his pants and undershirt again, with the offending pink shirt clutched in one hand, he reaches to push the linen shower curtain aside.

"Merde," he breathes. The utilitarian tub is half-filled, and half a dozen French-cuffed shirts are floating, bloated in the murky water, stained red with washed-out blood.

"*Jules*," he cries. "My shirts are supposed to be dry-cleaned!"

Two elderly gentlemen approach the ticket booth at the entrance to the lepidoptarium. One of the gentlemen is very large, with a broad, muscular chest and thick arms that belie his age. He is dressed casually, in gray slacks and a black mesh polo shirt. In contrast his companion is a compact, meticulous figure in an expensive navy suit with a pale blue shirt and a purple tie and pocket square. The ticket vendor is a bored young man, daydreaming in equal parts about sinking his teeth into a grilled hamburger and pressing his lips against the sticky lip-glossed smile of his girlfriend.

In French the smaller of the two men asks him how many other people are inside the exhibits. It is only ten a.m. on a weekday and these two men have arrived on the heels of a young couple, but the exhibits are otherwise theirs to roam undisturbed, the young man explains. The man wants to know how many workers are inside and where they are. This makes the ticket vendor pause, but in the end he explains that there is one other staff member on duty at the moment.

He must be inside one of the walkways, smearing treacle on the tree trunks to feed the butterflies.

The old man places a hundred-dollar bill on the narrow metal counter. The ticket vendor is surprised and even a bit suspicious of the large bill but he accepts it through a cut-out in the glass and begins to make change.

"Non," the man says.

Inside the lepidoptarium the wired-in sky winks through sparse trees. Delicate creatures descend upon Jules's and Jim's shoulders and arms almost immediately. They walk along the wide asphalt pathways, languorously trailing the young couple ahead of them into a pavilion. Before they enter the pavilion they hear a hushed rustling and look up to see a throng of yellow brimstones greasing the sky gold.

Inside, the two men separate. Jim stays near the couple.

"Did you know, sweetheart, that the ancient Greek word for the immortal soul, psyche, was also the word for butter-fly?" the young man stage-whispers in accented English into his lover's hair.

She turns her face toward him and says, "How wonder-ful, to have a butterfly for a soul."

The satyrs and nymphs of the natural world are laid out throughout the pavilion with encyclopedic dignity. From stubby caterpillar to deathly looking pupa, to magical scale-covered adult. The walls of one section act as screens upon which time and space are projected, vastly accelerated and magnified. Hushed voices, coming from speakers in the walls, narrate the exhibits. The screens display a pupa forming under the last cast-off skin of the caterpillar. Immobile, the ghostly outline of the butterfly begins to appear beneath the surface of the caterpillar's elongated casket. The feathers of the lepidopteran's head and body, the lineaments of its compacted wings become embossed on the surface. The chrysalis splits open in the last molt, and the adult insect crawls out, glistening wet and amorphous. Its dark body is swollen; its wings are crumpled. Grasping the branch beside the broken chrysalis, the bloated creature allows itself to fall upside down and hang while the body pumps fluid into the veins of its wings. The wings gradually expand and take on their crisp, decorated form. When the veins dry and harden, the wings may never be brought back to the body. Instead they stay outspread, flagging down mates until they become too worn and bedraggled to support the creature's weight.

The leather soles of Jim's shoes click softly as he treads at leisure. The couple are absorbed in each other. The man holds the woman against his side with an arm around her waist. She chatters to him enthusiastically about the half-inch wingspan of the pygmy blues and the even tinier span of the micro-moths.

In a room like a large cave, fat furry bodies fly about, robust in the semidarkness, chuffed between feathered wings. Silk cocoons from the giant Chinese silkworm moths are displayed in a softly lit glass case. Another case displays the uncanny death's-head moth, beside promotional stills from *The Silence of the Lambs.* The eerie outline of a skull decorates the back of the moth's oversized thorax. The death's-head moth feeds on nightshade and squeaks when handled. The woman squeaks as well when a tape recording of the moth's voice startles her.

Returning to the sunlight through the rotating doors, Jim blinks at the ache he feels when his pupils rapidly contract. Briefly obscured by the brilliant sun, the couple moves on down the path. He pauses for a moment. The air tastes powdered. A few glittering gold-and-blue butterflies have settled on his arms and hands. He lifts a hand slowly to eye level and examines the delicate, contracting wings of the insect clinging to his thumb. For a moment he loses himself in the irrational appeal of the long, dark proboscis coiled spirally beneath the enigmatic head. He wonders at the nebulous power of a body that can transport this weightless beast across continents but be snapped between two fingers of his hand. He pictures a long cloud of white pierids migrating through the sky, indifferent to the wind's direction.

And then he shakes his hand, releasing the insect, and he begins to stalk toward the couple.

Three feet away he clears his throat until they turn to him. The young man smiles politely. He smiles back. He reaches into his pocket, pulls out a weapon small enough to be almost concealed in his hand, extends his arm and fires a bullet into the woman's long, pale throat.

"Non! Non!" the young man screams, clutching at his lover as she collapses, dragging her up, lifting her lolling head with frantic, crimson-stained hands. "C'était moi que vous étiez censés tuer," he screeches. "Ils voulaient me tuer, pas elle. Pas elle."

Unaffected, Jim motions with his gun for the young man to release her. "Lâchez-la. Laissez-la partir," he demands. "Dis bonjour au diable pour nous."

Seated at the entrance on a bench reading the newspaper, Jules looks up when his companion returns.

"Jim, c'est fait?" he asks. "Ces papillons me rendent nerveux."

RAVEL

"So there is no 'language' of appropriation, because language itself is a system of appropriation. It's an entire world of mimicry that lies beside the real world, saying, 'I am your master. Because I have named you, even if you are oblivious to me you must be mine.' So the word for mountain owns the thing that is a mountain. Or, a better example would be that the word for a man owns the man, and changes him by placing him in a context. And the idea *context* is interchangeable with the idea *colony*. We take over what we understand. Because we don't give names to things to identify them, we give names to things to identify *with* them. Naming them is the first appropriation. That's the basis of economy. All an economy is, is a context. Economies are completely controlled by words."

Martine pauses to sip her wine. She fills the glass again from a bottle at her elbow. "The world doesn't distinguish between gold and silver, women and men, between diamonds and amethysts. But we do because we create names for them. And then the interface between the objects, the names, and all the language that evolves surrounding the names creates a context, and from within that context arises the discretion of an economy."

"What does that mean, Martine?" Guy interrupts. "How can you blame the words that describe what goes on in the world for what actually goes on?"

"I blame the words because they are guilty of creating the subject of guilt." She sniffs.

"Language isn't magic, Martine. Saying something doesn't make it so." He wonders why he raises his voice. The wine, he thinks, must be to blame.

"*Yes*, it does."

"*No*. It doesn't. I can say that I'm in Africa. I can say that you're a wallaby . . ."

"Then you would be in Australia."

"I can say that I never left. I can even make an argument that since my genes were here, in her . . ." He gestures toward Isabelle, who grins drunkenly. "But you and I and she and everybody knows that I was in Boston—not Africa, not Australia—Boston, which is only in one place, Massachusetts."

Guy shifts in his chair. His ass is beginning to ache; he has been sitting still too long. He feels a bit sick. His cheeks feel hot and the wine is beginning to burn his throat. Martine's lecture is getting on his nerves. He stares at the tears of light dividing the table. Moored by blackened wicks, the flames float in shallow pools of liquid wax. Across from him, Martine and Isabelle are lit by the wavering aura.

"Shh," Martine says. "We don't have to go over it all tonight."

"I remember the way that Sally used to set this table," he says quietly.

"Nothing matched, not the glasses or the plates or the cutlery or the candle holders. It all, somehow, didn't match beautifully, though. She could make a pot roast and serve it with a pizza and you'd think she had uncovered a new genre of cooking." Martine lifts her glass to eye level and studies the diffused candle flame shining through the wine.

"Where is she tonight?"

"She's dead. She died last year."

"I'm sorry. I didn't know she was dead. I mean, I noticed that she isn't here."

"We buried her out by the lake in the fall."

Guy looks over at Isabelle, falling asleep with her face buried in the gap between her crossed arms on the table. Martine watches Guy from beneath half-closed eyelids.

"Why did you come back?" she asks softly. She fumbles in her skirt pocket until she finds a package of cigarettes. She holds out a cigarette to Isabelle, who raises her head and reaches out. The cigarettes are hand-rolled, the paper printed with a green pattern. He tries to make out the pattern because something about the color seems familiar.

"Do you want one?"

"I don't smoke."

The women light their cigarettes by leaning into the candle flames. Isabelle coughs as she inhales.

"Mom," she says, yawning. "How long did Guy and his mother stay with you and Sally after his dad left?"

"Two months. We're talking about something else now."

Guy taps two fingers on the table. "Was it only two months? I thought it was a year or more."

"It was two months. Then we packed all your things and moved you to an apartment in Estérel, and sold your house to the province for the land."

"Over the piano shop."

"What?"

"The apartment was over a piano shop. And now I hate pianos. I was sure we were with you for a long time."

"Well, children often feel that months, or even days, pass like years. They only have a little time behind them, and your sense of time is always referential."

"You make them sound like dogs. Children aren't like dogs, Martine."

"How would you know? Children are, in fact, very much like dogs. They need food and water, company and affection, training."

"Mom," Isabelle interrupts, making a great effort to focus. Instantly, she forgets whatever she was about to say. Guy silently counts the empty wine bottles. Isabelle leans her head back down on her crossed arms on the table. She stretches one arm out, and at the end of her cigarette a pale growth of ash teeters, on the brink of collapse, over the tablecloth. He takes the cigarette from her hand. The green pattern on the rolled paper is a copy of the pattern on an American dollar bill. He puts the cigarette out on the side plate that Isabelle and Martine have been using for an ashtray. Martine's eyes narrow to slits of black light behind the smoke.

"Why did you come back, Guy?"

He shakes his head. "I expected you to be married," he starts. "I always meant to come back. I never meant to stay away forever." He stares at the wine, lying still in the glass. "When I left, at sixteen, I thought it was to make some money. But, all right, it was to run away. But I missed you, and Sally and my mom. My mother did okay, she eventually moved to Boston and started the second bookstore and wrote to me in Montréal and so I moved there to join her. I was working the coat check in a—in a gay strip joint. I'm not making sense, am I?"

He coughs with frustration. His vision is starting to blur and he blinks to clear it. "I missed you. I wanted to come back. I wanted to be responsible for the baby. I don't even know exactly why I never did. I thought about you all the time. I just never, I never, never got . . ."

"It's okay," Martine whispers. "I never expected you to take care of us. I didn't want your help. You were too young. Your mother did help. She was here when Izzy was born. She held my left hand and Sally held my right." Martine puts down her cigarette and folds her fingers into her palms and taps her knuckles on the table. "She and Sally used to take turns washing Izzy in the bathroom sink. It was your mother you hurt. Belle felt crazy without you."

"I know. She wrote me letters in which she said something to that effect. She died last month. *And* my job ended or, I guess, I ended my job. The woman I was seeing, well, it didn't work out. I thought at least"—he shrugs—"if I came and I didn't mean anything to her"—he looks at Isabelle—"no one could say that I never came back."

"I'm sorry, Guy. I'm sorry about Belle. How did she die?"

"Loudly, and with great resistance. She had a heart attack on her birthday. I stayed over the night before and we drank too much bourbon and spent the night singing, 'The Black Fly' and 'Un Canadien Errant,' until she went hoarse and I threw up. In the morning I brought her a chocolate layer cake with a whole box of candles, lit, in bed. She blew out the candles, fell back against the pillows and screamed. I carried her to my car and drove her to the hospital, but in Boston you always have to remember which hospital the patient's insurance covers. I took her to the wrong hospital, and she made me carry her out again because she could be so bloody cheap.

"We talked in the car while I drove to the other hospital. I think she had another heart attack, because she squeezed her breasts in her hands and her breathing got really strange and weak. I tried to hold on to her by confessing every secret I had ever kept. I tried to make her maternal instincts kick in by telling her all the bad things that I had ever done so she could hang on to give me hell. But it didn't work. She hung around to listen but then she went and had another heart attack anyway."

He shrugs. He doesn't like the look of compassion smoothing out Martine's features. He feels a shaft of bitterness thrust between a sudden longing for her mouth and the relentless unraveling of his memory.

"So, my mother died. My job ended. I couldn't face cleaning out her apartment. I didn't know what to do next. I don't know. Things just weren't going very well. It didn't seem like I could make it any worse. It seemed like a good time to come home and meet my daughter. I'm not staying. Don't worry, I'm going to take a short vacation and then start again."

Martine stubs out her cigarette in the busy mound of ashes and leans forward to blow out the guttering candles. A gentle scent from the burnt wicks rises with the smoke.

"There's something romantic about the smell of candles after they go out," Guy says.

"Come on. Help me carry Isabelle to bed. I used to do it myself but you missed all those nights. You can sleep in the front room. If you want to leave tomorrow, we'll drive you to the station."

The double bed in the front bedroom, pressed against the wall, used to be Martine's; Guy recognizes the spine of higher coils down the middle of the ancient box spring. He shifts his weight away from it. The window is open. A lamp beside the driveway illuminates the narrow yard, so bare. He blinks and imagines the old apple tree, pinpricks of stars shimmering through the ruffling leaves. He blinks again and the tree is gone. He squeezes his eyes closed and feels a sudden retinal flicker of memory—the hot white length of his mother with her back turned to him. Her long back in her nightgown, when they slept in this room together, years ago. Him, small beside her, watching her back, picturing her face, tracing with his memory the wet lines that streak her cheeks. For an instant he thinks that he catches a whiff of her skin. But then he realizes with a start that the smell of dry wood, fallen ashes and stale perfume that he has remembered for so long as his mother's youthful smell is the smell of Martine's house.

On the threshold of a dream, Guy rolls in the sheets until he is cocooned. The dream becomes more vivid and then the need to piss levers it down. In the end he rises to stumble through the darkened hall.

When he returns to the bedroom he feels nostalgia rising. Well, he feels something rising, and so he falls onto the mattress and stretches his sweating form, lying spread-eagled to let the breeze filtering through the gauzy curtains cool his groin and armpits. Sifting through a headache, a long memory plays back behind his closed eyelids.

Guy is nine and Martine is eighteen. This is ancient thinking. Their mothers, Sally and Belle, often take the kids to the beach with them, and so this is the first thing they do after Guy's father disappears. They pile the kids in the car and drive to the beach on a windy day, deposit their children in the sand and wander away to smoke and talk. Guy watches the two women walking away, arm in arm, slipping as they step.

Martine tilts her face up toward the sky. She pulls her shirt out of the waistband of her jeans and tucks it into the band of her bra, letting the sun at her long, white stomach. She stretches back to lean on her elbows in the sand. Nearby, Guy is picking up handfuls of sand and letting them fall slowly through his fist into a tiny cone between his feet.

"Hey, Guy, go back to the car and bring me one of your mother's beers," Martine murmurs.

"No."

"Come on. She won't mind."

"I don't want to go back to the car. You get it. Why don't you go with them?"

"Someone has to take care of you. Come on, go and get us both a beer."

"I don't drink."

She squints at the soft articulation of his young spine under his T-shirt. The wind raises blue-white peaks on the lake. The air is sated with the smell of wet things, seagull feathers, tumbled pebbles, maple leaves and crab shells. Martine's stomach still looks white but it is starting to burn. She pulls her shirt down to cover herself and closes her eyes. The sun on her eyelids plucks light tears into the fine net of her eyelashes.

The noisiness of the empty beach seems strange to Guy. When the beach is crowded, as it is on the weekends, all he ever hears is the clutter of car engines, radios and strangers talking. But this noise, the trees creaking behind him, and the lake rocking back and forth beneath the wind, makes his chest feel empty. The whole world seems to have a sound like the sound that his heart has to him, an undertone, more understood than truly heard, the uneasy noise of living.

"Guy," Martine calls out without opening her eyes. "I'm falling asleep. Don't run away while I'm gone, okay?"

A few minutes later her head falls against her shoulder and her knees teeter toward the sand.

In the distance, far along the edge of the sandbar, he sees the black outline of the rock outcropping where his mother and Martine's mother have escaped him. His days are long in the summer and there is so little to break up the time. He is forever being deposited somewhere, with someone, to be guarded as he entertains himself. He begins a silent monologue arguing for his right to spy.

His brown feet scar the sand, leaving pockmarks of evidence toward the rocks. Once he reaches them, he crouches. His mother and Sally have not gone far. They are sitting on Sally's favorite rock. It has a flat, wide table that never gets wet as the waves rush in. His mother only smokes when she is with Sally. He can hear them talking. He creeps up quietly between the smaller rocks, until he can position himself, shorts soaking wet, knees uncomfortable, at the base of the great slab.

His mother's voice is higher than Sally's but she coughs on the cigarette smoke as she speaks.

"I wish Guy didn't look like him. If I didn't see him when I look at Guy," she says, "I think I could forget him."

Sally tsks. "Don't worry, Belle. Guy won't be anything like his father. He'll grow up with you, and he'll be like you. He'll be kind and he'll be responsible and loving, like you."

"I hope so. But still, I think— Isn't it funny, the way your thoughts work so differently after something goes really wrong? When we fought over trivial things, like money or the house, I used to get so angry. I thought to myself, I have to get out of here. I imagined all the places and the people who could be in my life if I left, all the romances and careers I could have. But when things finally went really wrong I was so lost I only wanted to go back and forget everything. I would do anything to fix something so utterly broken, and I did so little to fix things while they still could be fixed. I used to scream at him that I wanted a divorce when he insisted on the house being cleaned three times a week, or having his dinner hot when he came in the door. I knew he had secrets. But this, he can't be the same person I had a child with. And I do remember him now, the way that he could be at his best."

"Men live in a different world. And those men, they live in a different world again. I know you're scared, but he's the one who's really lost. He won't get to see Guy grow, and he needs to, even if he doesn't think so now. Fathers need their kids. Sometimes we forget that until it's much too late. When Honoré left I cried for weeks. I know it's hard to believe."

"I believe it."

"I cried so much, Martine was afraid of me. Then much later she asked me if he had been real. She was speculating that he might have been a guest who stayed too long. Which I guess he was. My God, Honoré, he was just such a violently charming man."

"He was."

"There's something tremendously sexy about a really brilliant, really confident, really ugly man. I wanted to fuck him the minute I laid eyes on him, I wanted to fuck him every night for the rest my life. I prayed for years that he would just go. I knew I could never bring myself to voluntarily give him up. But I didn't want him to go, not when he was sleeping with other women, not when I was bailing him out, not when he was breaking the furniture, not when he was shaking me. I remember how sad I felt by the end, when we would have sex. We were fighting all the time. I pushed him away when he came to bed and he pulled me back, and at some point I just gave in. I knew he wasn't going to stop, and I didn't want to just be taken. It only took ten minutes and he sometimes still could make me come. It made me so sad to look at him, this man I loved."

"Honoré was never a nice man, Sally. He was too charming when he was charming, and he was too mean when he was mean."

"I know. But even after the worst of it I never thought, What have you done to me? I never thought about my poor body. I never even thought about Martine." She pauses. "I'm ashamed of it, but I just kept thinking, Where is the man I'm missing so much? What have you done to him? The last time I saw him—after weeks of waking up in the morning bleeding, my legs shaking, Martine still asleep—he followed me into the bathroom and put his hands on my shoulders, so softly. He sat me down on the edge of the tub and started brushing my hair. I couldn't say a word. I couldn't even open my mouth. I just cried. And all I could think was, Oh Babe, we're not going to make it."

"Why do we love them?"

"Because we can."

"Then why don't they love us?"

"They do. But, Belle, home is where you get your heart broken."

The next day Guy and Belle, Sally and Martine all ransack Guy's house looking for hidden money. Guy is in charge of turning his father's drawers over on the bed and looking underneath for taped bills. Martine is in the closet, searching in his shoes and rummaging through shoeboxes of cards and photographs. Sally and Belle are downstairs, turning over chairs and tapping the floorboards with their feet.

"Guy," Martine calls, "are you done with the drawers?"

He turns over the last drawer and his father's balled socks tumble onto the bed in black and white disarray. He scans the bare wood.

"Yes."

"Then come and help me."

Guy walks over to the closet and peers in. Martine sits cross-legged on the floor with a pile of photos on her lap. Guy sees a photo of himself in her hand.

"Don't look at those," he says. "Those are ours."

"I was there when that picture was taken. It was at a picnic by the lake last year. Mom took the picture."

"I don't look like that anymore. Put it away. Did you find money?"

Martine puts the photo back in the pile and begins to scoop them all back into the box. "No," she sighs. "He knew he was leaving. We'll only find money if he forgot it. You look in his suit pockets."

Guy steps into the closet and stares up at his father's brown and black suits on their hangers. "He didn't take any of his clothes because he's coming back."

"Maybe he is. Just look, Guy."

"He didn't hide any money because he's gone to get the money and bring it back. He has a bank account in London. He went there and he's coming back with lots of money. He said I could go to London with him sometime, and he would teach me how to drive on the wrong side of the road."

"You're too small to drive."

He opens the front suit jacket and stares at the lining. Bright silk shines under the light of the overhead bulb. He runs his hands over the slippery fabric. He gropes the pockets and finds them empty. On impulse he tugs the jacket off the hanger and pulls himself inside it. His father's suit jacket surrounds him, smelling warm and sick like his father, weighing down his arms and shoulders and the small naked nape of his neck.

———————

In the cool late morning they weave together across the beach, bumping hips as their feet cleave the sand. Martine hugs a thin jacket tightly around her rib cage and pushes her hair away from her eyes. Wind whistles loudly through the tree line. Twenty feet from the shore of Lac des Îles, a wall of fog amputates the lake. Waves slope back and forth.

"I want to show you where we buried Sally," she calls out.

"How did she die?" Guy calls back.

"She drowned."

"She drowned here?"

"No. She was in Nassau. She did some business there and then took a holiday, the first holiday I ever remember her taking. She was swimming in the ocean, too far from the shore, and she saw a school of jellyfish. They must have looked amazing, inflated tents of purple bodies in the azure water, shimmering strings trailing below. She had rented all this snorkeling equipment." She snorts with brief laughter. "Can you picture her?" She looks at Guy, and he sees that her eyes are streaming, from the wind or from emotion, he isn't sure.

"Yes," he says.

"She followed the jellyfish. If she had seen a shark with his mouth full of an accountant she would have followed that too. She just thought she was invincible." Martine covers her mouth for a moment. "Anyway, they stung her and she drowned. Someone found her, floating along. When the police called I argued with them. It seemed impossible that anything could take her down. I asked that she be cremated because she had a horror of being buried alive. So I never saw her again. They sent her to me all in ashes in this thin wood box that looked like it should hold cigars. The box came with an official certificate so that I knew those ashes were hers. I picked her up and brought her here.

"Izzy and our friend Harry and I tried to spread the ashes here, by this rock where she liked to sit. But the wind kept blowing handfuls of her back into my face. I just started screaming at everyone, at the world, just fell on my knees screaming and punching the sand. And Isabelle said, 'Mom, she's dead. There's nothing you can do.' I stood up and smacked her in the face. I couldn't believe myself. I know what you're thinking but that was the only time I ever hit her. I remember bringing Sally bags of ice for her eyes, and how much it scared me, and I never hit Isabelle before or after that. Anyway, we went back to the car and drove home and the next day Harry called some people, one in construction and one a stonemason. The mason carved her name on the rock table. The construction guy moved the rock away and then put it back after we buried the box beneath it."

She shivers, squeezing her arms about her chest. Guy studies her face. Her lips are dry and tight and her eyelids are dark.

"That night, I lay all over Harry, crying and fucking him for hours on and off. When the sun finally came up it all seemed so much like a dream that I felt happy again."

"How long did you stay happy?"

"Maybe as long as an hour. I knew it wasn't really a dream. Here we are."

Swirls of foam lap the base of the boulder. Only when Guy looks down at his submerged feet does he realize that they have been wading through the water. His shoes peek out from his pant cuffs like two straight black fish. He starts as she leans back against him. Her narrow legs are immersed to the calves. She lifts her skirt up, twists and squeezes the hem, and then tucks it into the front of her underwear. She lifts her feet up, one by one, removes her sandals and tosses them onto the table. She climbs in two wide, careful steps.

"It's the rain," she calls down. "The water's not usually this high. Do you remember this rock? Your mother used to sit up here and smoke with Sally."

"Yes."

"Come and sit with me." She reaches out.

On the rock his hand grazes an unnatural shape. Sally's name, half-obscured by his palm, is carved in roman letters. He watches Martine trace the *z* in her last name with her index finger. Chazal—the name that transformed Sally Anders of DDO, a muted suburb of Montréal, into Mme Honoré Chazal of Ravel, a one-house town hidden in the upper Laurentians.

"It was hard for them to do this. It's not an even surface. Put your head down on the rock. You'll be surprised how much it feels like hugging Sally."

Walking back through the forest with Martine stepping quietly beside him, Guy draws calmness from the air.

"What did you do with Isabelle when she was little?" he asks cheerfully.

"What do you mean?"

"Did you walk her to school? Did she like to skip rope? What kind of games did she play?"

A branch snaps beneath her instep. "Sally and I kept her at home and schooled her until high school. We used to bring her to the beach to swim after studying. She liked to splash us. I have pictures I can show you. We swung her between us by her hands. We chased each other around the trees and sometimes we'd all climb together. We played with Isabelle the same way we played with you when you were really little."

"She didn't have any friends?"

"She had us."

"Before my father left," Guy says, "my parents used to swing me by the hands between them when we went for walks."

"I don't remember much about my father. I only remember things about my mother from when he was around."

"My mother once said that they used to go to movies with your parents and it was embarrassing because your parents kissed beside them for the whole movie."

"That's hard to imagine. But Sally never slept with anyone else, as far as I know, after she met him."

"Maybe she loved him even after he was gone."

"She was a lot stronger without him."

"She must have loved him."

"I don't know anything that would make me think she should. I don't know what she thought about him. She never gave up her married name, even though Sally Chazal always sounded like a mix-up. But she never taught me French. I know, I speak it, but only what I learned in school. I never think of it as my father's language. Sally was strong on her own. She couldn't have been strong if he had stayed."

Guy inhales roughly, shaking his head and sucking on his front teeth. "What's it like to be so tough?" he says. "You don't contain an atom of romance, do you?"

"You think he deserves romance?"

"I heard your mother talking once. I think that she kept on loving him. Didn't you ever think that it might be nice to fall in love with one person for your whole life? It might be *nice* to be someone's only love, someone's only lover. If that part of your brain could be filled with one face then you'd never have to compare it to any other face. You'd always know, walking and talking and sleeping and eating, whose eyes and nose and mouth you'll see when you turn your head."

"You're not talking about my father."

They continue losing step in silence. The chirping of squirrels sounds dissonant and frivolous. He watches her lips purse and he thinks how red they are, when she wipes her hand across them.

"Are we going to air all our grievances at once?" she says at last. "You're wrong. I did care about you. It just wasn't the most important thing."

"What was the most important thing?"

"Having Isabelle."

"And having your own life."

"I never thought that it could be anything but my own life."

He closes his eyes but he does not stop walking. He has a sudden vision of himself as a thin, white boy diving into an icy lake, penetrated by needles of panic. He clears his throat and then clears it again and tries to voice something calmly.

"It doesn't hurt you that I was gone, does it?"

"Guy, stop it. You left. I didn't make you leave."

"I'm not like you. I can resign myself to the world as a place where you lose things for a specific, good reason. But I can't resign myself to the world as a place where you just lose things. The way you say things, Martine, you make everything seem meaningless."

She begins running. Her skirt flickers behind her like a flag. The air gathers a sudden weight and she stops. The clouds simmer above them in an unexpected agitation of thunder. Guy feels something on his cheek, and on the top of his head, and then he hears the whisper of raindrops rushing across the canopy. Martine stands far ahead of him with her head thrown back and her palms raised to the sky. He treads through the instant night. She turns to look at him when he is a few feet away. Her face is wet.

"Guy," she says softly. "Your hair is getting wet and your shoulders are getting wet and your face is getting wet."

He stops. "Martine," he says. "Don't do this to me."

"Guy, your neck is getting wet. Your legs are getting wet and your hands are getting wet."

"Please." A wooden finger turns in a space in his mind. His erection is already full and his stomach is churning. "Don't play games. Be fair to me."

He can feel the rain rolling in rivulets down his cheeks and the back of his neck and over his hands. He blinks away the drops gathering on his eyelashes. He licks his lips. He blinks again and sees Martine, glowing by some preternatural energy in the shadows. Her face is flushed radiant, her naked body is sketched by her wet clothes. He catches himself staring at her breasts, imagining their weight in his hands, and drags his gaze back up to her dark hair. But from there it travels to her white neck, slips over her narrow shoulders, around the sharp curve of her waist, down her hip.

"Martine," he whispers. "I waited so long for you. I waited so long to touch you. I tried to grow up fast. Every time I thought I had stopped wanting you, you would do something, and I would break right open again. I waited so long it was unbearable. And when you finally wanted me it was to get pregnant. It still wasn't me you really wanted."

"Don't you say that, Guy. It isn't true."

He stares at her fingers unbuttoning her shirt. He stares at her round shoulders as she reaches behind her back to tug at her sleeves and pull her shirt away. Her round, low breasts appear, tipped with amber nipples. Her skirt is discarded, and he stares at her softly belled stomach, her long, thin navel, and the brown curls of hair in a narrow V between her thighs. He hears her speak and he tries to listen.

"I did want you, Guy. I really did want you."

Her open hands stretch toward him at the end of elaborately long arms. Her open lips fold over his. Her chin is in his mouth. She puts her hands on his shoulders and pushes him to his knees, backs him onto the ground. They tumble together to free him from his clothing. Her eyes burn impossible iolite blue as she rocks him between the thresholds of labia and lips, between the warm, muscular walls of her vagina. She moves him into and against her harder than he dares. The nub of her breast is between his teeth. Her hand cups his testicles, fingertips trace the ridges. Sticks and pebbles pit the heels of his hands as a deep thrill builds. He pushes his mind away, trying to hold on. Over the scent of the rain-sopped pollen and dirt laden with feathers, seeds and the turds of small animals he finds the scent he seeks. He finds the clear, warm honey in a pan on the stove scent of Martine's cunt. There it mingles with seawater stillness, the comforting, conclusive scent of semen.

When they are exhausted, together in the mud, with only Martine's skirt pulled over them, the rain stops. He brushes away bits of leaves from her cheeks and tries to wipe the mud from her hair. She stares up, the glassy shivering wind illuminated as it scatters water from the leaves. He starts to say something, but she covers his mouth with her hand. A few seconds pass.

"Are you cold?" he mutters through her fingers.

She nods and crushes against him.

He raises himself on his hands and tries to roll over and cover her more completely.

"You're too heavy," she laughs. Her head is tucked against his neck; he feels her breath when she speaks. "We have to go back to the house soon."

"Do you want to climb a tree with me?" she says. She sits up, pulling her skirt off them. She stands and begins to pull her streaked clothes over her painted skin. She wipes her mouth with the back of her hand.

"That's a good tree for climbing," she says, pointing to a tree with large low branches. "Isabelle and I both like climbing that tree."

Martine walks to the base of the tree and begins climbing. Guy's gaze follows her.

"Martine," he calls up to her. "Where did you get that scar on your stomach?"

She continues climbing. "Come on, climb the tree with me," she calls. She is already fifteen feet above him.

He stands, recovers his pants and pulls them up. He steps onto the first branch and begins to climb. Martine has gone much higher than he had expected.

"I don't think this is safe."

She ignores him and he climbs. She stops and moves around to the other side of the tree to wait for him. His shoulder muscles are not used to being pulled like this. He breathes heavily until he comes abreast of her. He feels especially vulnerable with his naked torso held against the hard bark. He begins to wonder if he will be able to get down again. She reaches out to put her hand over his hand on his side of the tree.

"Don't look down," she whispers. She leans her body around, swinging herself to reach him. She pulls his lower lip between her teeth as she kisses him.

"I don't want to climb any higher. Martine, I want to get down."

"Guy," she says. Her pupils have eclipsed her irises.

"I'm going down now," he says. She catches his belt loop and hangs on to him. "Martine, we're going to fall. Hold still."

"Okay. Okay. But you stay then. I'll hold still if you stay here."

He looks down and almost loses himself. She squeezes his hand. This high in the tree the shadows make it hard to see her face clearly, but her teeth shine when she smiles. With her free hand she tucks her hair behind one ear and then behind the other and then she reaches over and wipes his forehead. They are smiling at each other as she reaches down and he feels her carefully handling his zipper, then wrestling with the brass button in its buttonhole. She leans her face close to his and slips her hand into his open jeans and grips his penis. She masturbates him carefully. He tries not to move. Martine's hand has him, moving up and down very gently.

He feels his body's lurching ambivalence. His legs start to shake. She brushes his stomach with her knuckles. Almost losing her footing, she leans in to kiss his mouth. She slips her soft tongue between his closed lips and squeezes his penis more firmly. He breathes deeply as she kisses his mouth and his cheek. He puts his arm around her waist to hold her more securely against the tree. A pensive heat gathers along his thighs. The soles of his bare feet ache on the branch. He adjusts his footing and leans into her embrace. Looking up, he sees a small patch of open sky between the lacework of black branches. A long minute passes. A bird with white underwings and red wingtips crosses the sky between the break. Guy squeezes his eyes shut. He feels himself coming in her warm palm and he steps back.

"Guy!"

He hits three branches with his arms and legs on the way down. It takes a long time to hit the ground. The pain in his foot when he crashes with his full weight onto it, and it crumples like paper on fire beneath him, is the most shocking thing. The pain begins but is cut short almost immediately by unbearable hot numbness.

"Guy! Guy, are you all right?"

"No!" he yells back, hanging on to his leg with both hands and rolling back and forth on the ground.

He hears the dull thud of Martine's last little jump to the ground. Her voice sounds muffled. "I think your leg is broken. Does it seem broken to you?"

"Yes!"

"Can you walk on it?"

"Shut up! Just shut up for a minute."

"You stay here. Don't even try to move. I'll run back to the house and get Isabelle."

"No! Get an ambulance."

She sits back on her heels and looks at him. "I think we should wait here for a few minutes until you can stand and then I'll help you walk. If you lean very heavily on me, I think we can get you home."

"I don't want to walk!"

"Don't yell at me. I could leave you here."

"Martine."

"I'm not going to. I'm just pointing out that you won't get anywhere with me by yelling. I know you're in pain, Guy, but if you can just ignore it enough to stand and lean on me, I'll get you home. I can run for help but it will take a long time and I can't leave you here like this. Just wait. I know, I'll make a splint."

"Please, just shut up. Go get an ambulance."

"This isn't a real road, it's too narrow for an ambulance. Hang on."

She rushes away, and Guy alternates between moaning, swearing and calling her back. She comes back with two long sticks and tries to straighten his leg. He screams, lurching up and shoving her off him.

"There, you see, it's much straighter now." Martine sticks her finger in a small tear in her skirt, worrying the hole until she can tear the material. She begins tearing off strips from the bottom of her skirt and bracing his leg in place between the sticks. Guy pants and coughs, kneading his forehead with the heels of his hands. His skinned back stings.

"Do up my pants," he groans.

"Yes, of course. Come on. Stand up. You'll be all right. Shh, shh, shh. It's only half an hour to the house and then I'll call a doctor."

"Just sit with me a minute, Martine. Please, just sit here quietly."

"Can we go now?"

"You're all dirty." Guy smiles a foggy smile.

"I think I had better go for Isabelle."

"Do you remember that story Sally used to tell, that fairy tale about the woman in the forest whose husband died?"

"No."

"Yes. It was this sad story about a couple. This young woman's husband was a forest ranger or a lumberjack, and he died in an accident. You remember?"

"A lumberjack?"

"Yes. I think something bad happened with some kind of tree. After he was buried she walked away from the funeral into the trees. She walked and she walked and when she found the center of the forest she sat on a rock, and she said out loud, 'I can't believe my only love is dead. We were young and nothing was missing. We made love all the time. We had a nice home. We were good companions. We agreed on all our plans. *Still*, it wasn't enough. How can I go on when it doesn't matter to the world how much you want something, how happy you are, or how much you're loved?'"

"Guy."

"Wait. Just listen. She lay down on the ground and decided to stay there until she died too, from exposure, or from starvation. She decided not to move, to just think of him and wait until the pain ended. So she didn't move for days and then for weeks. The leaves gathered over her and the wind blew them away and they gathered over her again. The rain and the dew slid into her mouth and kept her from dying of thirst. On the twentieth day her husband finally appeared to her, sitting on a rock nearby. He looked at her and he didn't say anything. He just sat there looking at her until she started to cry. Then he disappeared. She cried through the night and through the next day. Then, the next evening, she finally sat up and said to the rock that her dead husband had been sitting on, 'I'm sorry, I can't stay here anymore.' And she went back to the village and she got on with her life. She married again and had a family and she buried other friends and older relatives. For the longest time she felt terrible regret that she couldn't will herself to death for grief, but after a while she discovered that she was basically happy. As happy as she had been when he was alive."

"I don't remember that story."

"I think it's a story about how love always fails. Love always ends and the lovers always survive. I was sure that Sally told it to me. I can almost hear her voice when I'm telling it."

"You sound like you're in really bad shape. Come on, stand up. I'm taking you back to the house. I'm worried we've stayed here too long."

"Did you have sex with Martine?"

Guy lies in bed. His leg and hip are tightly wrapped in makeshift bandages torn from old curtains by Martine. Someone sits with Guy.

"Who are you?" He looks carefully at the young man's unsmiling face. He can't be more than twenty-four. He has blond hair and wide, calm eyes, and his large hands are open, palm down on the bed.

"I'm Harry. I live here. I didn't want to meet you, but now it looks like you'll be staying awhile. So, did you have sex with Martine? I only ask because it's not uncommon for men to come home with injuries after having sex with Martine." He leans closer to Guy, reclining slightly on the mattress. "You know, the first time I had sex with Martine it was in a park."

"Look, whoever you are, go away," Guy stammers. "You don't have to tell me about this."

"I'm Harry. Yeah, I know I don't have to tell you. Anyway, I barely knew Martine, she was just Isabelle's mother, and I came to the park to see Isabelle. She liked to read on a blanket in the grass. I was hoping to catch her feeling sweet. We were talking for a while when Martine joined us. It was a gorgeous hot day and the three of us went for a walk. We stopped for a while to watch a school archery practice." Harry pauses. The way he smiles makes Guy groan.

"I guess at some point Isabelle walked away. Martine was standing in front of me and we were watching the arrows. She leaned back and slipped her hand down and grabbed me. Then she led me, without letting go, into the trees behind the targets."

"She's got a thing for trees," Guy interrupts, shifting uncomfortably. "Where is she?"

"She's downstairs, calling an ambulance. So, there we are leaning against the tree trunk, Martine has her skirt bunched up to her waist. And suddenly a stray arrow hits me right in the back of the shoulder. I shout, and this shower of kids breaks through the bushes to see us flagrantly fucking against a tree, and I have an arrow in my back. Very mythological, don't you think?"

Guy clears his throat. "Do you think the ambulance will be much longer?"

"Are you in a lot of pain? The second time— Am I boring you?"

Guy shakes his head meaning yes, stop, but suggesting, no, go on.

"The second time was under a truck in a parking lot. I don't know why, I had a car parked a few feet away. I guess I liked the desperation of it. The pretense that it must be now, not in five minutes, not tomorrow, not in a bed, someplace less painful, just drop to the ground, roll under the truck and fuck."

Guy groans. "Harry, I'm sorry we had to meet like this. But I don't really want to hear any more about you and Martine. I don't care."

"Don't you? Well, if you're not already lying and you really don't care now, then you will. You'll care when she falls asleep. You'll care when she goes for a walk with someone and then calls you hours later to help her because he has a crushed foot or a broken pelvis, or a gunshot wound or something. It's not because of love, either. It's the foolishness of it. It's you seeing the light that was in you when you were the one hanging upside down, or swinging from something, or crawling into some strange place, seeing that light in someone else. He feels it like you did, all hot and clean and overpowering. As if you couldn't do anything wrong if you did it with her. You'll see that light and you'll feel humiliated because it will look stupid to you when you see it in him."

———————

The trip to the hospital blurs into dull imaginings, awkward bumps and pain. They spend three hours in the crowded waiting area before the doctor finally X-rays Guy's leg and finds several bones broken in his foot but nothing wrong above it. The bones are set. The foot is encased, and the drive home disappears behind his weighted eyelids. Eventually he is home again and he falls vertiginous into sleep.

When he wakes, the suffocating night and the pain in his leg pin him to the bed. The floor seems miles away. The window is open. He can't remember what has happened, so he feels for his leg and finds the hard plastic of the cast. The house is full of people laughing and then the house is silent. He thinks Sally comes in with his mother and then he thinks Martine is sleeping beside him. His chest aches, and his dry eyes burn. The street lamp shines through the branches of the apple tree in front of the window. His father's suit jacket is draped over his legs. Martine breathes warmly beside him, her body slight and tender with sleep, emanating a singular heat. Her blue eyes shine through thin, closed lids.

Guy looks out at the apple tree. "I thought it was gone," he whispers. The white blossoms glow against the Prussian blue of the branches. Each blossom glows individually, and then he notices that each cluster of blossoms has a more yellow glow, and each branch of blossoms suffers a redder radiance against a striated violet sky.

Martine rustles quietly, like a cat in the sheets, and she whispers, "Guy, if I said that I love you, and that I'll only ever love you, would that be the only thing I ever had to say?"

"Yes," he exclaims, exasperated.

She holds his hand tightly, tightly. The house begins to shake as he slips from his hallucination back into sleep.

He has one proper dream. He dreams that he is scaling the side of a mountain. The mountain is very sheer and he has no shoes. The rock face is limestone and the sky overhead is flat and clear. Every foot he climbs, he passes some strange sort of animal fossilized in the mountainside. At first the squiggles and crescents and tuberous shapes seem familiar, one could be some sort of anemone, there a broken fern, under his hand the spine of a sea plant. And then Guy sees what looks like the frayed end of a lobster's tail. His foot hurts. His hands feel weak.

His knee brushes something: a bird, flattened out, as if it flew into the rock and stuck there. He looks at the sky and feels dizzy. He looks at the sea and feels sick. The rock face is soft, touching his cheek. He climbs slowly, feeling a strange weight around his neck. The weight runs down his back and past his feet. He looks at the rock beside him and sees something so big and so skeletal that he stops climbing. He can't make out what it is. But he can see something that looks like a hoof and the extent of the fossil suggests that it could be the size of a deer.

"I'm climbing this mountain with no equipment," he says out loud, astonished. And then he realizes, just as he realizes that up ahead is an even larger fossil, and a shadow creeps across the sun, that the sweet weight on his shoulder is a drape of rope and that he is not climbing without equipment. He is climbing with a noose around his neck.

TADOUSSAC ET BROMONT

In the morning Jim slits a man's throat and lets the body fall into the magnificent fjord. He stands on the steep cliff looking down at the churning sea, playing with a pack of matches. He pictures the body rolling in the waves, between the white bodies of beluga whales making summer love in the lower Saguenay.

He lunches on the patio of a small auberge on gratin d'escargots aux bluets. The sweet flesh of the snails is smothered with blueberries and cheese. The waiter combs a tablecloth and asks him if he desires coffee. On the street in front of the patio a young boy struggles to sell umbrellas to the suntanned crowd.

"Rose, bleu, mes parapluies! Parapluies de Fendi," he cries. "Préparez-vous pour la pluie!"

By midafternoon he is in Bromont, following an adult English class through the gates of the Safari Loowak. He strolls behind the last pupil, listening to the light voice of the instructor. A woman in the group snatches the hat of a man and places it on her own head. Jim shakes his head and whistles. A woman in a man's hat is always a sign that something dirty is about to happen. He studies his nails while the instructor explains the safari and invites her students to practice their English in conversation. Serge Poirier, she explains, the famous butterfly collector, created this safari to make adventure games and treasure hunts on his five hundred acres of land. There can be horse riding, she explains. Or search-and-rescue games around the wrecked aircraft hidden in the trees. Many companies bring their executives to play these adventure games, she says.

In the sun-scorched field ahead someone is being guided at gunpoint into a red helicopter missing most of its metal tail. Dappled horses graze in the field nearby. Men in identical drab suits stand in the grass gesticulating.

"Look," the English teacher says. "L'enlèvement du président. Après moi, the president is being kidnapped. Now his executives must make a rescue."

The woman in the fedora looks over the scene. "Sont-ils censés être du Front?" she speculates.

"Please try the English," her teacher cajoles.

"Are they meant to be the FLQ?"

"Non. I believe they are from a competing company, maybe."

Inside the forest they come upon the fuselage of a smashed biplane. The couple with the hat chase each other around the angled wings. She climbs in the seat and mimes a takeoff while he pretends to be Superman, flying beside her. The class watches with amusement. The teacher clucks fearfully when the man climbs on the wings and stands erect.

Jim wanders in the shade, drawing on a thin cigar. He checks his watch and shakes some coins in his trouser pocket. The man and woman hold the group's interest while he leans against the trunk of a red oak, smoking.

In another clearing is another broken plane, another English lesson, another lovers' game, another smoked cigar. But here something is different. As he studies the group he has a sensation of nerves tingling in his back. He turns around. Only the trees are behind him. But the feeling of being under surveillance does not go away. And so, because there will be another opportunity to kill the man and woman in the night, he silently extracts himself and walks back toward the cabin for an espresso. The winding path is strewn with treasure maps. The sandy earth mutes his footsteps. He stops. Another set of footsteps stops. He takes his lighter from a pocket, shakes another cigar from the pack and raises it to light. The broad, mirrored surface of the lighter reflects only the path and the forest. He spins slowly, rolling his gaze up and down and around the immediate terrain.

A few minutes later he pauses again to pry wild raspberries from a bush. Again he notes an echo. He waits.

"Avez-vous les yeux de rayon X?" he calls out.

Silence.

"Avez-vous les yeux de rayon X?"

He dashes in between the trees. As he runs he smiles; at last he hears his pursuer clearly. He breathes heavily. The next clearing opens in front of him and a young man almost smashes into his back when he suddenly stops. The broad clearing is stocked with ravaged jet fighters. Three dark hulks face each other down in a simulation of a Mexican standoff. Each one is twisted and split into monstrous mounds of metal. One plane is little more than a cockpit. The nearest plane is riddled with holes where the sunlight shines through in narrow rays.

He turns; the man is young and poorly dressed. "Avez-vous les yeux de rayon X?" Jim says.

"I don't understand."

"Do you have X-ray eyes?"

"No."

"That's too bad. Then you can't see what I have in my pocket for you." He draws the knife and holds it up to show the young man. He sees the narrowing eyes, the pursing lips of someone deciding not to show fear. The cruel blade is rusty with the morning's work.

A sly expression crosses the young man's oily face. He tilts his head and purrs, "But I only thought you might be lonely out here, in the trees. I was going to keep you company."

Jim snorts and puts the knife away. He waves a hand, dismissing the vile creature and his furry smile. "Go back to the streets. I am a married man," he says.

RAVEL

"Do you want some more Demerol, Guy?" Harry asks.

"No. Did the doctor give me Demerol for my foot?"

"No, it's Martine's. She didn't want you to be in any pain. Can I have it, then?"

"Go ahead."

Sleep nets him again. Hours later, when he shakes awake, he sees the room in snatches, his thoughts still tangled in the drug. The white sun streaks the dirty bedroom window; waxy red cherries roll in a blue glass bowl tilting in the cream sheets; and Isabelle lies in a paisley sundress at his side.

"Are you finally awake?" she whispers without opening her eyes.

"Yes. Are you?"

She murmurs, nods and stretches her arms over her head. The whites of her eyes look very clear.

"Harry said some awful things to me," he complains.

She shakes her head. "Don't listen."

"Is he in love with your mother?"

"Yes, no, maybe. I don't think so. Now that Sally's dead I think I'm the only one left who loves her." She yawns. "I was thinking that we could go camping together. We could borrow Harry's car and drive up north. I'd like to see a bear."

"You and me and Martine?"

"No, just you and me. To do something together, to father-daughter bond. You came back for me, didn't you? You didn't come back for my mother?"

"No, you. Of course I came back for you. But I can't go camping with a broken foot."

She eats the cherries from the bowl. Her lips are stained dark red from the juice. He sighs and stares at Isabelle's feet at the bottom of the bed.

"You have feet like your mother's."

"Do you think so?"

She lifts her head and turns her feet back and forth to look at them. "My feet are longer and my toes are farther apart than hers, I think. She has small feet with tight toes. I think my feet look like yours."

Guy wriggles the toes sticking out of the cast.

"The other foot."

"Isabelle, why don't you tell me something about yourself?"

"What would you like to know?"

Guy shrugs. "I don't know. Tell me about school or tell me about your friends."

Isabelle laughs and stretches. The stippled flesh of her armpit releases a baby-powder scent. "I can tell you about my first lover." She looks at him closely, gauging his reaction.

"I was thinking more along the lines of your childhood. You have your mother's . . ."

"I have my mother's what?"

"You have your mother's way about you, your mother's boldness. Well, that—okay, if you want to talk to your father about your first love, then he should listen."

"I'll keep it fairly clean. I was sixteen. I used to sit in the field and read after school and he followed me after class to tease me by asking me what I was reading, and wouldn't I rather see a magazine he had? One day he sat down beside me, pulled out a book of his own, lay back in the grass and started reading. I said, 'Excuse me,' and he said, 'Shh, I'm reading.' So I said, 'Suit yourself.' And we read like that until I got up and went home and he stayed there reading.

"He started lying down beside me to read every day and then he started bringing us two Cokes to drink. They were so cold and sweet. I pretended to read while I waited for him to arrive and then he walked me home afterwards and we talked about our books. It was fun to talk to someone my age about books. He liked William Burroughs and I liked Milan Kundera. He liked Franz Kafka and I liked Gabriel García Márquez. We both liked Knut Hamsun, and D. M. Thomas. He liked Henry Miller; I don't think he was concentrating very hard when he was reading Henry Miller.

"Anyway, when he lay down beside me I wanted to lie down too, but I couldn't quite. Sometimes he took my book away and read a page or two out loud to me and then said, 'Wow, pigtails,' or 'Wow, poor dog.' I tried to take the book back from him but he held on to it for a minute before letting me have it. Sometimes he read me a dirty passage from the book he was reading and then looked at me and said, 'Well, what do you think of that?' and I said, 'I think you'd pass out.'

"One day he was walking me home, telling me all about *Tropic of Capricorn*, imagining himself as Henry Miller; he could barely walk straight. All of a sudden he whispered in my ear, 'I think I'm going to touch your hair,' and I said, 'Go ahead.' But he kept walking. Then he said, 'I think I'm going to put your fingers in my mouth.' I said, 'Go ahead.' But we kept walking. He said, 'I think I'm going to kiss your eyes.' I said, 'Go ahead.' He said, 'I think I'm going to squeeze your breasts.' I said, 'Go ahead.' He said, 'I think I'm going to lay you down and put my mouth on you. I think I'm going to carry you into the shade and have sex with you. I think I'm going to fall asleep on your chest with your hair in my mouth and your skinny arms around me.' And then he picked me up and I started laughing, so he put me down, and I said, 'Oh, don't.' So he picked me up again and ran with me over into the trees.

"We had sex in a fog of mosquitoes, in the shade of a huge tree. Afterwards, he looked over all my insect bites. He took a lemon out of his knapsack and sliced it in quarters. He ate one slice like it was an orange, and then offered me one. Then he squeezed the rest of the lemon juice onto his fingers and dabbed it carefully on all my bites, and the stinging and the itch went away. We just couldn't stop laughing."

Guy looks down at his daughter lying beside him on the bed. Her hair shines on the pillow. He feels himself blushing.

"What happened after that?"

"Nothing."

"You didn't read together anymore?"

"Yes. For a little while, and then he was off following someone else."

"That was your first love story? He betrayed you."

"It's a funny story; it's not a love story. Do you know what Mom says? She says that you should never be anyone's first love. Nobody ever forgives their first love."

Isabelle leans on her elbow and spits cherry pits into her palm and then drops them in the bowl. She wipes a small red stain in the center of her palm against her skirt. "Now you tell me about your first lover."

"My first love or my first lover?"

"Are they two different people?"

"None of your business. You kick your feet a bit when you laugh. Are you sure you don't want to talk about how you did at school? Or what you want to do when you grow up?"

She wipes her mouth with the back of her hand. "Nope," she says. "I know how I did at school. And I am grown up, ta-dah. Now you tell me about your first love. Tell me what it felt like. Do you still miss her?"

"No, I don't miss her. So maybe it wasn't real love." He coughs and moves away from Isabelle slightly. A face, a favonian little face hovers in his memory, slipping in and out of focus. "I do remember what it felt like. It felt like I had a rabbit in my heart and sand sifting in my head. It felt like I could go blind with wanting to be near her." Guy pauses. "I don't like to remember what I used to think about love when I was little, about what it would be like to be a man. It makes me feel disappointed about all the heroic things I never did."

"You could still do them."

"No. My darling daughter, that's what you learn when you grow up, being a romantic hero is virtually impossible because almost anything that you actually do— Well, most things are only heroic in the dreaming of them."

"You're depressing me." She falls on her back on the bed beside him and stretches.

"I'm sorry. Okay, if you insist, I'll tell you about my first attraction. I was about six or seven. It was a cloudy day and I was walking quickly away from my house to get out of my mother's sight. I knew she would call me to stay inside because it was going to rain. I tripped and skinned my knee. I sat down on the sidewalk and looked at my blood and then I leaned over and licked my knee to see what it tasted like. I heard someone giggle above me. I stood up and there was this little girl standing on top of a pile of wood in front of an unfinished house. Her hands were on her hips and her legs were spread so that the sun shone through them, and she yelled at me, 'I'm Wonder Woman!'

"I said, 'You are not.' And she threw a rock. It hit me in the eyebrow and I was so surprised I sat down again. 'What did you do that for?' I said. 'Because I'm Wonder Woman,' she said. 'Do you want to play? Because if you want to help me conquer the Bahamas we have to run around my house five times and then jump in the pit and hide.' So I said, 'Okay,' and we ran around her house.

"When we had run around the house five times we were

breathless. Her face was sweating. She leaned on her knee, hiccuping, and said, 'Okay, now we have to jump in the pit.' She showed me a hole in the backyard where they must have been digging a pool. I stood at the edge and she ran up behind me and pushed me in, and then jumped in after me and landed on top of me. I was so mad that I pinned her down. Just when I was pinning her down, and she was laughing, I looked at her face and her teary, scrunched-up eyes, and for the first time in my life I felt this weird happiness. It was just a tickly warmth in my belly. Then she bit my arm and it started to rain."

"I like that story."

"It feels good to have one easy love story."

"My mother says you were always like this."

Guy looks across at her looking at him.

"That you were always kind of sad and optimistic."

Guy smiles. "My father left when I was very small. I always thought he would come back."

"That's funny," Isabelle says. "The same thing happened to me."

Isabelle leans up on her elbow. Her little nose reminds Guy suddenly of Martine's nose. He feels a bit sick with nostalgia.

"Did you ever fall in love?" he asks.

She shakes the cherry pits in the bowl. "Falling in love is for other people. I think it's one of those things that are meant for the rich. Like swimming with sharks, or jumping out of perfectly good airplanes. People like me don't want to fall in love."

Isabelle hears something outside the house as she descends the staircase. She slips on her sandals and opens the front door. The sharp knocking is repeated. It is coming from the side of the house. She walks around and sees Harry chopping wood. The muscles in his jaw knot under the golden shimmer of his damp skin. His hair is plastered in white tendrils to his forehead. Sweat rolls down his neck. His blue shirt is black against his chest, and at the folded circles beneath his swinging arms.

"Harry?"

He stops and looks over at Isabelle. He puts the ax down beside the chopping block and throws two halves of a log aside. Pieces of wood litter the grass.

"Why are you chopping wood in the summer?"

He shrugs and sits in the grass and the splinters. He breathes deeply and bends his head. "How long is he staying?" he asks finally.

She sits down beside him. She squints up at the bright, flat sky. She covers Harry's long fingers with her own and finds them wet.

"Is he coming to Ste-Famille with us? What does he know?"

"It's going to be okay, Harry. We still need you."

Hot water tumbles out of the faucet into the bath. Martine leans her face into the steam, inhaling through her nose. She kneels by the tub in her skirt and bra. Several days have passed since the accident, and Guy is relieved that she is going to help him take a bath. He washes his face and underarms with a cloth at the sink every morning but he can smell the warm grease from his scalp on his pillow, and his back and chest and legs feel sticky and hot when he wakes up. His foot doesn't hurt but the skin inside the cast itches so wildly that he has to smack the cast with his fist to get any relief, and then the relief is only that his hand hurts enough to distract him.

"Don't do that," she says. She looks at him over her shoulder and smiles. "You're lucky it was tarsal bones that you broke and not the tibia," she says, wiping her hands on an apricot-colored towel lying beside her. "Also, you're lucky nothing was displaced. You'll be fine in a few weeks." She gets up from the floor and walks over to Guy. He pulls his T-shirt over his head and she grabs it to help him.

"I don't need help with my shirt," he crabs at her.

"Okay," she says, backing away with her hands raised. "Can you do your pants too?"

"Yes. I wish you hadn't ripped them," he grumbles, referring to the long tear along the seam, ankle to knee, that Martine made in his jeans to fit them over the cast.

"I'll sew them up again when you're better," she says. "It's not so bad. Your cast looks like a ski boot. These plastic ones are so much better than the old plaster casts." She watches him stand and brace himself against the wall to unbutton his pants and then sit down again to pull them off. He hobbles over to the bathtub and stares in silence, as if he is checking for dangerous fish. After a few seconds of consideration, Guy pulls down his underwear and seats himself on the side of the tub. He struggles with the underwear, caught on the cast, and reaches to grab a plastic bag and elastic bands from the floor. He pulls the plastic bag over the cast, affixing it with the long rubber bands. Finally, he slips into the tub backward with his foot held up so high that his head goes under. He rights himself with his hands and sits up coughing.

"You have very pink testicles," she whispers. She opens the medicine cabinet and takes out a pink bar of soap and a green bottle of shampoo. She squeezes some shampoo onto his hand and lets him vigorously scrub his hair.

"Where were you yesterday?" he asks, finally. "I only saw you at breakfast."

"I was working in the basement."

"What were you working on?"

"A project about time and the accumulation of meaning."

"You're writing a book?"

"No." She sighs. "I was joking. It's a different kind of project." She pulls her legs up to sit cross-legged on the floor. She offers Guy the soap. "I would have just put the soap in the tub but I was afraid you would drop it and hurt yourself."

He scrubs his shoulders, catching the soap in the shampoo lather and dragging them both down his arms. Martine reaches over to take the soap from him and scrub his back. Her confident hand rubs circles around his neck and down his spine. He feels as if a huge bag of sand across his shoulders has been torn open and the weight of the sand is leaking away. He leans forward to let her scrub the base of his spine under the water. His back and his uninjured leg and his groin ache from the effort of accommodating his immobilized foot and ankle.

When she finishes with his back she presses him against the bath wall and soaps his chest and stomach. He catches her hand as it slips below the water but then lets it go. She soaps his legs and his thighs gently. She soaps between his toes and rubs the balls of his one foot with her thumbs. She soaps under his knees and draws the water up in her cupped hand to splash the soap away from the knee that is raised out of the water. She soaps his hips and then his genitals, dipping under to clean his buttocks.

"There," she says, handing him back the soap and standing up. "I'll get a bowl to rinse your hair."

He closes his eyes. The water has cooled off or his skin has warmed up so that now he finds it difficult to detect the exact boundaries of his body. Just as he feels himself falling asleep, he sits up to keep from slipping under the water.

Martine returns and fills a bowl with water from the sink. She puts the bowl on the floor and kneels down beside the tub again.

"Martine, where did you get that scar?" he whispers.

In the daylit bathroom he can see her skin better. The scar is just below her ribs in the middle of her stomach. It's straight and silvery beside the smoother whiteness of her unmarked skin. He reaches out and touches it with his wet hand. It puckers and draws the underlying flesh with it when he presses with his finger, suggesting that the damaged tissue goes deep. "Were you in an accident?"

She lifts the bowl of water from the floor and pours it over his head. Guy shakes his head. She puts a hand up to block the water spraying off his hair.

"Take off your skirt and come in here with me."

She smiles and stands. She unzips her long skirt and rolls off her socks, black men's socks, he notices.

"They're soaked anyway," she says. She reaches behind her back to release the catch from her silk bra, and Guy is struck by how beautiful her breasts are, low and full beneath freckled collarbones. Her nipples are much larger than they were when she was twenty-six. She steps out of her underpants and into the tub. Guy tries to move his leg out of the way, but she has to lift it up herself, ducking under the cast to seat herself. Their bodies are oddly locked and yet not intimately connected at all.

"I can't reach you," he complains. "I'm stuck."

"That's okay," she says. She takes the soap from him and begins to scrub her shoulders.

Guy watches her for a second and then says, "Tell me what you were doing yesterday. Why don't you answer my questions?"

"Because I don't want to. I don't think you would understand." She scrubs her arms and her underarms.

"Don't use that adult-talking-to-a-child tone of voice with me."

"I'm sorry, it's an old habit. Okay, then, I *am* writing a book. It's detective novel. I'll recite the first line for you: 'The detective turned up his collar and frowned.' Guy, I want to ask you to do something for me."

"Okay."

Martine leans over to scrub her feet under the water, and then her tiny ankles. "I'd like you to go away for a while."

"What?" His gaze snaps to her face.

She smiles. Her nose is sweating. "I want you to take Isabelle away for a while and spend some time with her before you spend too much time with me. Okay?"

"I just got here."

"I know. But I need you to go away again. I have a lot of things to do and I don't want you around while I do them."

"What do you have to do? I won't get in the way. Is this because of Harry? Who the hell is Harry, anyway?"

"He's our friend. Isabelle wants to spend time with you, and yes, I want a little time with Harry to explain you."

"But I have a broken foot." He sighs and tries to move his leg around her but only succeeds in knocking her in the head with his cast. "Sorry," he says. "That was an accident. I didn't mean to hit you."

She grabs her ear. He slings his foot over the side and stands in the tub. The water level abruptly sinks. Martine looks up at him as she washes her breasts and her stomach.

"I'm not sending you away for good." She releases the soap in the water. "I want you to come back afterwards."

"I knew you would want me to bring her back, Martine." Guy pulls a towel from the rack and wraps it around his waist. He grabs his walking stick from the doorway and hobbles out of the steamy bathroom, away from her. Outside the door he stops and listens to her splashing. He turns around. "I'll take Isabelle away tomorrow," he says, "if you'll tell me where you got that scar."

Martine stares back at him. Then she sniffs, closes her eyes and leans her head back until her hair and her ears are submerged in the bath. "I stabbed myself in the stomach one day when the world seemed full of noise. Is that what you needed to hear?"

Isabelle wants to eat before they set out and so she is in the kitchen, making sandwiches. Guy watches Harry check off on a list in his hand the items he puts in the trunk of the car. Tent, sleeping bags, bellows for blowing up the mattress, bellows for blowing on the fire, inflatable mattresses, ax, tarp . . .

"When did you make that list?" Guy asks him.

Harry looks over at Guy. "It's just a standard list I keep on the computer. I run it off every time we go camping. Do you have a bathing suit?"

"No." Guy turns away from Harry's sudden friendliness.

"I can lend you one. Martine's packing you a bag upstairs. She probably already included it."

"I don't think I can swim in my cast." He stares at the window on the top floor of the house. It irritates him that Martine might be packing Harry's clothes for him. "Harry," Guy mutters, "what are you going to do when we come back again?"

Harry sighs, tucking the pen behind his ear and placing his broad hands on his hips. "What makes you think I have to do anything?" he asks. "What makes you think that just because you decided to come back everything is going to change?"

"Where's your own family?"

Harry shrugs and sits down in the grass. "Why? I have seven sisters in New Brunswick. They all have kids and pets and jobs and husbands. I'm eight years younger than my closest sister, Jane. My family doesn't need me."

"Where are your parents?"

"They both died in a car crash when I was four. They were hit by a drunk driver, pushed off the highway. It was a terrible crash. Even the tape in the cassette player was destroyed. My mother's maiden aunt, my great-aunt Beth, finished raising four of us, the four oldest went to live with friends, and then Beth died too."

"How did you come to Ravel?"

"I wanted to see the country. I traveled around after my aunt died. I went up north when I was seventeen to plant trees. When I wanted to go home I called my sister Jane and her husband told me she was pregnant again. He said I should look for a job in Montréal or Toronto and then he wired me some money. I just wandered around the townships picking up work until I met Isabelle, reading in the park, and then Martine took me in. I met Sally and I told her I would leave in the morning. She said, 'You can stay as long as you like. You can have the front room. Your poor mother would cry if she knew your sisters didn't take you in.'"

"I can picture Sally saying that," Guy says.

Harry looks suddenly fatigued. He hasn't shaved in several days, but the sparseness of his pale beard only emphasizes his youth.

"Lunch is ready," Isabelle calls from the door, waving. "Come in, come in!"

L'ASSOMPTION AU PARC
DE MONT-TREMBLANT

They drive into the Camping de la Tête section of L'Assomption as the afternoon slides into evening. They find their site and Isabelle sets up the tent while Guy broods in a lawn chair by the car. The campsite backs away from the road and onto the forest in a deep bottleneck. Thick rows of rock maple and sugar maple block the other sites from view, but the chattery French singsong of children debating the ratio of hot dogs to hot dog buns filters between the trees. Isabelle unpacks the car and begins preparing dinner from the baskets in the trunk. She sets an open package of butter tarts on the picnic table and smiles at Guy.

"Are you hungry? After we eat and rest for a while, we can go down to the water and swim."

On the shore of Lac des Femmes, Guy watches Isabelle swim away and then kick and turn and swim back to him. The splash of her stroke sings clearly in the quiet dark. Guy leans back in the coarse sand and wriggles to get more comfortable.

Opening his eyes to gaze at the uninterrupted sky, he feels dizzy. White strands of constellations braid across a black desert. Below, the reflected stars glimmer, twinned in the flat water. He inhales and notes a new depth to his lungs. Mosquitoes provided white noise at the campsite while they ate and while Isabelle stacked wood beside the fire pit. But down here, by the water, the breeze is too strong, so the air empties, and the distance between Guy and all other things in the world increases.

He looks up as Isabelle falls down beside him. She takes a deep, sharp breath and whispers, "God, the sky is drenched with light." She settles in beside him, wrapping her slight body in a turquoise bath sheet. She sniffs and rubs her nose with one corner of the sheet. "It really does look like a dome. I mean, you can see the curvature of the atmosphere. The water is still warm. It's too bad you can't swim with your cast. It would wake you up and make you feel all clean and happy. My muscles feel wonderful." She raises her feet up one by one and flexes them in the air.

He turns and looks down at Isabelle. She has her arm behind her head, and her glistening eyes look enormous over her wet cheekbones.

"Why choose L'Assomption?" he asks. "This is the most remote section of the park."

She sniffs wetly and licks her lips. "That's why. It's quieter here. Diable is too popular. You can do everything in L'Assomption that you can do in Diable, but without feeling watched."

"Your mother writes books?" he says, changing the subject. "She must have done well. Has she always worked at home?"

"Yes," Isabelle says. "But she doesn't write books. I don't know where you got that idea. And we make all the money together."

"How do you do that?"

Isabelle grins. "Well, I make the paper, Mom prints the bills, Harry does the embossing, and we sell it all once a year in July, in Ste-Famille."

Guy can't seem to hear clearly. "You mean—? No, I have no idea what you mean."

"Yes, you do. Your mother was the first woman Sally helped. Mom told me you were there when they searched your house. Your father didn't leave any money behind but he left a checkbook for an account that your mother wasn't involved with. Your mother stayed up all night with Sally, practicing his signature, and between them they forged a check for twenty thousand dollars. Your mother cashed that check to start her business."

"The bookstore."

"Yes."

"No. *No!*"

"Don't yell."

"Don't tell me . . . No! Sally lent her the money. Sally was famous for helping women in Ravel after their husbands hurt them or abandoned them. She did it because . . . because she understood. Because your grandfather was so violent." He shakes his head, insistent. "My parents and your grandparents were friends. They met in school. They went to the same parties. They knew the same people and they . . . Honoré used to hit Sally, and my father hit my mother. He even hit her in front of me once. He hit her across the face for laughing at him. Christ." Guy pauses. "I think that's my earliest memory."

The domed sky crenellates with northern lights. The fire crackles at their feet. She stirs the flames with a long stick and he watches the end of the stick begin to glow. It might be midnight but it might be four o'clock. An animal rustles in the bushes. The mosquitoes have disappeared. The crowded sky cannot brighten any further. A liquid ripple of colored light contracts the stars inside a spiral. He watches his daughter in the unsteady aurora of the campfire. The world seems too impossible for morning.

Dreaming, he hears Martine's voice calling him back to the past, "Guy! Guy! What are you doing here?" Her voice stutters with laughter. There is a boy beside her, laughing as well.

He stops running and looks down at his shoes. His feet are very small. One of the thick black shoelaces has come undone, and when he tries to hide it behind the other foot, he loses his balance and falls into the sand.

"Come here, you clumsy flamingo."

Her tall silhouette, framed by the sun, strides toward him. She crouches to face him and smiles.

"Did you follow me all the way down to the beach from your house?"

She is wearing her black-and-white gingham bikini. Sand dusts her breasts and stomach and the front of her thighs, wherever her skin touched the ground after swimming. Her long hair sweeps forward and touches his knee.

"Were you spying, Guy? Were you listening to me? Spies are tortured when they're caught." Grabbing him, she scrunches her fingertips under his arms until he shrieks and falls against her. Falling back in the sand, she pulls him on top of her and tickles and tickles as he pleads.

"Martine, let him go," the boy says. "Tell him to go home. Tell him we need privacy."

"That's right." She sighs and lets Guy go, but he holds still against her, picking up her hands and attempting to make her tickle him again. Her skin is cool and damp and gritty. "You have to go, little spy. Why don't you come by our house later and we'll play checkers." He clings to her hands. "Can't he stay?" she calls to her companion.

"No. Come on, Martine."

Guy stays silent.

"You can stay if you don't mind what you see. Won't it gross you out, though? To see us kissing?"

He breaks away from her.

"Guy! Where are you going?" she yells as he runs away, down the beach, across the sand, ignoring the sharp stones tearing the soles of his feet. He runs and runs.

He halts by the large rocks. Sally's rock is ahead of him, and he decides to climb up and lie down on top of it. He struggles to fit his feet onto small protuberances so that he can climb. At last he braces his hands on the table and hoists his body up. The sun heats the rock's surface. Looking across the lake, he sees the low shadow of another town skimming the horizon. A seagull screams as it floats in the air. He stares at the bird. The sun signals off the white wings, creating the illusion that the bird's feathers are aflame. He leans back. He spreads his arms and legs out so that his calves and his feet hang over the edge of the rock and his hands are in the air. He purses his lips and whistles. An image of Martine flickers behind his closed red eyelids. She is sitting at the kitchen table across from him picking up a red checker and leapfrogging it over three black checkers. He feels happy to be playing with her. He likes it when she laughs at him. Her laugh sounds like his mother's laugh, only higher and happier. Her bleached hair reminds him of lemonade; the sun makes it so bright. Her breasts in her bikini top remind him of snowballs, tight and white.

Yesterday, Guy caught a frog. It was a thumb-sized brown frog with little red bulbs on the ends of its toes. He put it in the plastic baby tub his mother keeps in the garage. He put some water in the bottom of the tub, and he pulled some grass out of the lawn for it to eat, and floated the broken grass in the water. He covered the tub up with three sheets of blue paper towel so that the frog would think this was the sky and not remember that he was in a baby tub in the garage. He feels excited about showing Martine the frog. He decides to give Martine the frog and then he sits up and scrambles down the rock to go and tell her about it first in case she doesn't want it.

Hiding in the trees just above the sand, he can hear Martine laughing. He peeks out from behind the trunk but he can't see her yet, so he threads a little farther down the beach. A branch snaps and he listens for her boyfriend to yell at him to go away, but no one hears him. At last he sees them, lying a few feet away. Martine is on her back and the boy lies between her legs with his stomach against her stomach. She lifts her head and kisses him. The boy reaches between her legs and slips his hand into the bottom of her bikini. Blood sears Guy's cheeks. He swallows. He wants to run but he can't move or they will hear him. He holds his breath and then lets it go. His legs start to shake and his nose starts to itch. The boy undoes Martine's top and the triangles of fabric fall into the sand. He kisses her neck and he kisses her breasts, and he moves his hips against hers.

Martine turns her head and looks back, toward the trees. His heart pounds. He can see the boy's hand moving between her legs. He can see the boy's fingers disappear. He can see the flush spreading across Martine's breasts. Her nipples point to the sky. She squints and twists her head a little more and then she smiles. She shakes her head and the boy removes her pants and then his own trunks and enters her. Martine looks toward Guy and then closes her eyes. His knees unlock and he turns and scrambles away. He flings aside branches and kicks the long grass. Horrible buzzing insects chase him. He runs through the trees and his heart shakes his chest as he stumbles and rights himself and continues to run. He reaches the road and stops. He touches himself, touches his own neck and chest. The hot asphalt shimmers like a ribbon. He starts to cry.

Guy wakes to the disturbing sensation that he is buried up to his neck in sand. The sun is high overhead and he is sitting in the lawn chair, covered with a canvas tarpaulin. His eyes sting from the sweat and the ashes caught in his lashes. Isabelle sits across from him, sipping from a steel mug.

"Does your face itch?"

"No. Why?"

"You have mosquito bites."

"Thanks, now it itches something awful."

"Sorry. Here, have some coffee." She holds her mug out to him, and then laughs. "It's okay, it's just coffee. Were you dreaming about your mother? You were making noises in your sleep." Her voice is soft with sympathy.

"No, but I was dreaming." He sips; the coffee tastes strong and nutty. "I was dreaming all night, I guess."

"No, you weren't dreaming. I really told you about the counterfeiting. I really am a counterfeiter. It's a beautiful day, we could go swimming. I could hold your leg up for you in the water if you want. Are you hungry?"

"Listen to you." He throws off the tarpaulin, upsetting his chair and standing up with amplified dignity. *"I'm a counterfeiter. What do you want for lunch?"*

"Are you mad at me? I didn't do anything wrong."

Guy punches his cast and scratches his face. He can feel a hot braille across his cheeks. "You told me that my whole family were criminals and my daughter is a felon but you didn't do anything wrong. Fine, great, wonderful news. How do you—? What am I supposed to feel?"

She takes the mug back from him. "We don't really say felon in Canada. Relax. You knew about your dad, and your mother wasn't a criminal. She only committed one crime and she did it to take care of you."

"How do you do it?"

"We scan bills into the computer and manipulate the image with PhotoShop. We blow the image up and go over it carefully to clean up every detail. We use a jeweler's lens to go over the bill for comparison. How much do you want to know?"

He doesn't answer her and so she continues. "If you photocopy money you lose the resolution, and it always looks too shiny and feels too smooth. That's why amateur counterfeiters get picked up so easily. But we go over every millimeter, and then we draw on the screen what we see in our hands. Harry is the color expert. Matching inks is difficult, but Harry can do it. The U.S. plans to introduce more colors into their bills soon but that won't be any problem for Canadians to counterfeit; we're used to multicolored bills. So, I make the paper with cotton and linen scraps. I boil the scraps until they fall apart, and I add some shredded one-dollar bills. The paper has to feel the same. You'd be surprised how important it is for money to feel right in your hands. I build a strand into the paper that identifies the bill's value. We get those strands on spools from the dealers—I guess that part of the bill is for real."

"Christ, stop it. No. All right, tell me."

"Are you sure? Okay. Then Harry and Mom print it and etch it. We batter the dry bills, scrunch them up and scratch them with dry pens and coins, and leave some in the sun. We spread it out in the backyard and put stones on the bills to keep them from flying away. We do all that to fade it so that it looks like it's been on the market for a while. There's more to it, of course. You look really sick. Are you okay? By the time we finish it's the same, really, as any money."

Guy clears his throat. "Except that it doesn't correspond to anything of value in the real world. It doesn't represent anything."

"Yes, it does, as much as any money. It corresponds to the work we do." She shrugs. "And it corresponds to the expectations of the people who handle it. What else does money represent?"

Isabelle digs her feet into the sand and wriggles her toes to loosen the mound that covers them. "The days when coins were worth their weight are long gone," she says. "Mom always says that you have to destroy the economy, that you can't participate in the economy as if it's money that makes people equal. It's money that makes people *un*equal."

Guy stares at her profile, her tilted face and lowered eyelids.

"We, and by we I guess I mean they, the Federal Reserve," she says, "we only make money so that something neutral can be with invested with any meaning. Money is supposed to stand in for the meaning of things. But . . ." Her voice sounds increasingly tinny and distant to him. "Let's face it, work is so distorted from the value of money paid for the work, that even the paper representation is starting to disappear. It doesn't matter that one woman smashes bricks all day for a living and another models silk pajamas. It doesn't matter that there is enough of almost everything, food, medicine, shelter in the literal world. You don't have to think about it now that it's only numbers. It's too hard to argue about it because it's too hard to imagine what the numbers really mean. It's easier not to look. You don't have to print the numbers out if you don't want to. All the transactions are becoming invisible as they move further and further out of the grasp of the people who have no money."

Guy is silent for a minute. He shifts in his seat, gestures for the coffee. "What about the people you are involved with, aren't they dangerous?" he asks carefully.

She wraps her arms around her chest. "We only deal with them once a year. They knew your dad and Mom's dad. Sally went to them for help after your father left."

"Our fathers were smugglers. They had friends who were thieves, or killers."

There is a long silence between them, and when Isabelle finally speaks a strange quaking in her voice knocks him off guard.

"You think I'm a criminal like your dad and his friends. You hate me now?"

"I don't hate you."

"Are you going to leave again?"

She slips into the tent to escape his silence, and he starts a fire. The day draws in around them. Suspended outside the ring of smoke and heat from the fire is a low, buzzing curtain of insects. Although his legs and face are too hot, he does not want to move back. Finally the air chills with the threat of rain, and the insects depart. The wood is almost gone but he puts on another log. His thoughts are tangled in white noise. Guy looks at the rows of tree trunks and imagines a wind coming down from the stars. The air feels heavy and wet. He has a sudden vision of Martine crouched in her basement, her hands and arms covered in green ink, a jeweler's glass scrunched into her eye socket, surrounded by hills of cash.

Later, they go to the beach even though it is raining. Warm drops pit the sand. They have the long question-mark-shaped beach and the gray waves to themselves. Isabelle undresses with her back to Guy. She steps into her bathing suit and pulls it up and strides to the water. Watching her long spine reticulated beneath her lovely skin makes Guy shiver with discomfort. She stands at the water's scalloped edge and kicks the waves. The lake looks huge and dark. He holds the umbrella over the lawn chair and himself and digs his bare toes into the thickened sand. Isabelle moves into the water slowly. She treads with care, her arms held out for balance. The water must be cold and the lake floor must be stony. Somehow she has a dark shimmer of threat concentrated around her neat limbs. He tries to pressure his emotions, to see her as something more innocent. Watching her, he feels an unhappy nostalgia for his father. He tries to shoo away the rising memories and imagine her simply as his daughter, a girl swimming in the rain. He concentrates on her small shoulders bobbing beneath the surface of the water, and on her long hair floating around her face. Her face, neck and shoulders all look small enough, pale and polished enough, at this distance, to belong to a child.

She looks back at the man on the shore. He holds his umbrella so close to his head that it functions as an enormous hat. The rain pricks her back with silent fingers. On the very surface of the water, if she watches closely, she can see the water drops explode. Each tear-shaped drop hits, breaks into a tiny cup and collapses. She closes her eyes and dives to touch the underwater ferns. Under the surface, Isabelle feels clean again. She rolls and her hair floats about her cheeks. She puffs her cheeks out to feel them fill. A strand of grass enlaces her fingers. Her skin tingles and grows numb. She emerges with a gasp and Guy is standing at the edge of the lake without his umbrella.

"Are you all right?" he calls.

"Yes," she sputters. "Yes, I'm coming out now."

"I thought you were drowning." He shuffles awkwardly. The rain drums over the water as she wades to shore.

She spends the afternoon hiking through the dripping forest alone. Lashing at the bushes with a stick, she whistles tunelessly at the fragments of sky that appear like a flickering film through the interstices of the branches. Several times she hears rustling in the bushes around her. Occasionally a small toad skips across the path. In a clearing she stops and listens. She hears water rushing over stones. She follows the auditory path until the noise seems overwhelming, but its source is still invisible. Broken boulders, stacked taller than her shoulder, block the water from view. She climbs the rocks carefully and when she reaches the top she sees a waterfall, tumbling down into a narrow river. The trunks of pines lean perilously over the eroded bank. Spray from the waterfall dampens her hair and she feels suddenly thirsty. Splashing, the sound of someone splashing arrests her attention. She has seen campers in their campsites, and in the washrooms and on the beach, but her forest ramble has been strangely solipsistic. She squints at a figure a few meters away, knee-deep in the rampant white rush. The figure is too rounded and dark to be a man and yet he seems like a man.

The bear keeps his head down and swats with a square paw at the shallow pool spanned by his legs. Isabelle holds her breath. He looks irritated, she thinks. He looks like Guy. The bear lifts his head and swoops his nose up and down in the air and she can almost see his nostrils dilate.

The bear rears up on his hind legs and casts a shadow the length of a car across a frill of fish rendered suddenly visible by a movement of the clouds and a sudden engagement of sunlight with spray. He brings his body down in a final furious splash and then turns and ambles away. His backside rolls with the weight of his hips as he treads on thick limbs to the riverbank.

Guy has scratched his face to bleeding when she arrives at the campsite. Hunched under the tarpaulin, he swings his head to look at her. His cheeks are spotted with ash.

"I saw a bear. Help me, I want to put some food out for him. What do they like? Do they like butter tarts or bread? I've never seen anything so huge. He was fishing. It was just amazing to watch him concentrate."

"Stop!" he squeaks, and then regains his normal voice. "Put the food back. My God, Isabelle, what color was the bear?"

"He was black but he had a blond snout. Why do you want to know what color he was? He didn't see me but I think he could smell me. I followed him into the forest but I couldn't find him again. I had this feeling watching him that I was so happy I could fall down and die right then, it would be okay. I felt like I had suddenly fallen in love. I've never felt that way before."

"Are you out of your fucking mind? Put the butter tarts back in the cooler. Put them back, back in the cooler! For God's sake, listen to me, Isabelle, it could have killed you. Come on, I'm your father. Doesn't that mean anything?"

She stops arranging the food on the picnic table and wipes the back of her hand across her mouth. "I would play dead if he tried to attack me," she says, defensive.

"How do you think it would test if you were dead? It wouldn't take your pulse. What do you know about bears?"

He stumbles to stand. The campsite grows claustrophobic with the encroachment of an invisible bear.

"I know that teddy bears were named after Teddy Roosevelt."

"Teddy Roosevelt *shot* bears! Please put the food away. There are children nearby."

"But it was beautiful. You don't understand. Listen to me, Guy. I saw something special. It was this huge animal, alive in the place where it lives, and I was there too. I heard it splashing in the water and then I saw something that I wasn't supposed to see; I saw a live bear, relaxed and fishing. It was incredible. It was the best, Guy."

He feels himself giving up, feeling utterly helpless to stop her from crumbling leftover food in a trail along the campsite. It won't come here, he thinks. It probably won't come out where all the people are. He closes his eyes because he can't stand to watch her. After a few minutes she comes back to the picnic table and takes out bread.

"Are you hungry yet?" she asks.

"Yes."

"Okay, I'll make a sandwich for you too."

He collapses with a frustrated grunt into the lawn chair and pulls the canvas tarp around him. "Can we compromise? What if we leave the food out for an hour and sit very close to the fire and then in an hour we'll clean the whole thing up again?"

Isabelle eats a slice of cheese. "Okay, but an hour and a half. You know, it's strange to see something just living like that, without a job or some kind of trick to get out of having a job."

He remains stoic, ignoring her for a minute, but then because it feels like this is the first normal thing she has said in days he asks her, "Do you want a job? Because I could help you find a job."

"No, I don't want a job. Having a job is just like accepting your punishment for being alive. The less valuable your life, the worse your punishment. That's why women are paid less than men. That's why minorities are pushed into labor positions."

"You don't think men get punished for being alive?"

"Well, you get punished too. I mean, men like you do have jobs, but you're more likely to get retirement packages. For women and minorities, work is pretty much a life sentence. What do you do?"

He sighs and scratches his forehead. His hand comes away wet and sticky. The swirls of his fingerprints are stained with blood. "I was a social worker," he says, wiping his bloody fingers against his shirtfront. "But I don't have a lot to say about it. I don't want to do that anymore. I'm looking for a new job."

"Were you a good social worker?"

"No, I was lousy. I had four clients commit suicide last year and only two of them were suicidal when I started visiting them."

"That must have been hard. Isn't that a risk for social workers?"

"With other social workers it's a risk."

Isabelle laughs quietly. She cuts the sandwiches in quarters and puts four quarters on a paper plate for Guy. She brings it to him and then returns to the table to collect the other sandwiches. She lays them end to end on the ground in a line. Finally she takes the last sandwich and sits in the empty lawn chair on the other side of the fire.

"It's nice to hear you being funny," she tells Guy.

"I'm not being funny. This is true. This is my life."

"I know. That's why it's funny. Do you work at a shelter?"

"No. I work on a task force dealing with high-risk families. I started a program the first year I was there to give computers to high-risk households, you know, single-parent, low-income families, poor areas of Boston. I got businesses that were upgrading their systems to donate their old computers for a tax credit. I thought it was a great idea. I was so excited, bringing the computer to the kid's house and setting it up, and teaching him how to use a basic word-processing program to do his homework. I felt like this great guy, like Santa Claus. But then I'd go back the next week and the computer would be gone and one of the parents would tell me there was a break-in. I knew there was no break-in. What was I thinking, teaching a kid to type over the sound of his stomach rumbling?"

"It's not your fault. It sounds like you tried to do good things."

"Yeah, well. I tried doing intervention work with alcoholic parents. But they were always saying to me, 'Do you have kids?' What could I say? I could lie, say no, and then they wouldn't want to listen to me give them advice. I could say, 'Yes, I have a daughter but I've never met her.'"

"Do you have a girlfriend?"

"No. I did have someone until recently. But I brought home this guy, a recovering heroin addict. I thought if he stayed with me for a week I could keep an eye on him and keep him straight. She left with him. They totally stripped my apartment. I'm just not good with people. I can't tell what's going on in their heads. My life," he starts and stops. "It's a mess. It's just not working out."

"Look. There he is," Isabelle whispers.

In the serrated shadows at the forest periphery something large moves. The breeze shifts and Guy smells the dirty wet-straw scent of the bear's fur. The bushes part, and the bear strolls into the campsite. He lifts his square head and Guy briefly holds his intense, brassy gaze, out of shock, before he remembers to look away.

"Don't move, Isabelle."

"He's so lovely," she whispers.

The bear sniffs at the chain of white triangles and steps forward with impossible cautiousness. With his head lowered, his shoulder blades form a sharp peak atop his monumental matted back. His long muzzle is gilded with pollen, ending in the dry slate of flaring nostrils. The birds fall silent. Even the smoke above the fire seems frozen in the air. Guy feels a constriction in his chest as he hears his breath whistling out.

"It's okay," Isabelle whispers.

"Please, don't talk to the bear."

"It's okay. I think you're beautiful," she whispers to the bear, holding out her hand and crouching.

"Stand up, Isabelle!" Guy shouts.

The bear draws his body up to a semi-stand. He sniffs the air and growls. His voice vibrates in the air. Isabelle keeps her hand extended but she stands and sways on her feet, in unison with the bear.

"Look, we're dancing," she whispers.

Guy's throat is so tight it feels as if his fear could hang him. He moves beside Isabelle, slowly, slowly. The bear snorts and loosens his shoulders to show the breadth of his chest. Sharply curved yellow claws decorate his massive paws. Guy puts his arm around Isabelle's waist to hold her in place and he raises his other arm to make them appear like one very large, very brave being. The wind rises and the wet leaves glitter like shattering glass.

Suddenly the bear drops to all fours and charges toward them. In the few seconds when the black bolt rushes from the green background Guy somehow releases Isabelle, reaches the canvas tarpaulin, turns to the bear and snaps the tarp open. It falls like a tan parachute through the air between them, and when the sound of it falling heavily to the ground clears from his brain he sees that the bear is gone.

"I want to go home."

Isabelle ignores him, chattering happily about the bear as she tries to make more sandwiches in the rain.

"I think I'm going to make room in my religion for angels, and all the angels will be bears. We'll make bears to go on top of Christmas trees and bears to watch over our beds."

"I want to get off this campsite."

"Relax. Help me make more sandwiches."

Guy scowls at the struggling fire. Raindrops pop on the smoldering wood. He stirs the base, and flames flicker but then instantly abate. "I can't keep the fire burning in the rain."

"Did you see his eyes? I looked right into his eyes. They seem so tiny underneath that massive forehead, but he has this gaze, incredible."

"Isabelle, do you know anything about bears? Do you understand that he would have hurt you, at the very least, to get the food? How can you be this naive? How can you be so criminally naive? Is this some, some genetic problem, a combination of my nervousness and Martine's apathy?"

"Are you going to keep trying to build the fire in the rain? You know it's going to go out. Mm, this honey tastes great."

"They're not herbivores, if that's what you think. They're omnivorous—they'll eat anything. Bears have even been known to chase down humans and kill them for food. And it's not a nice way to go, with a three-inch incisor through your eye."

"It's raining. The bear is at home in his cave. There are lots of people at the beach in the day. Look how close we came to him and nothing bad happened."

"I want us to sleep in the car tonight and we'll drive home as soon as the sun comes up. I would leave now if I could drive, but I can't with this stupid cast, and I don't want you driving in the dark because you obviously don't have an adequate sense of safety. Take the sleeping bags into the car. Lock all the food in the trunk. I'll put out the fire. You can go swimming in the morning, but only if there are more than ten people at the beach. But then you promise to drive us home!"

Isabelle stirs in the backseat, almost falling, and then lies still again. She dreams of tomatoes ripening green to gold and splitting to release a flow of diamonds. She dreams that she and Guy are bear cubs knocking each other about in the water, splashing until tiny fish spray into the air. Guy opens his muzzle and snaps at the spray. From the shore she hears her mother's voice. She turns and waves but sees only the black bear. She wades to shore. The bear lies on its side, breathing laboriously, eyes rolling in their sockets, mouth snapping open and shut as it whimpers.

Guy snores and shifts in the passenger seat. He kicks his feet, feeling shrink-wrapped in the sleeping bag. Sweat rolls into his eyes. In his dream he swims through the lake at night. Waves lash his face and obscure the shore. He gasps for breath, feeling that he is swimming too slowly. He kicks, desperate to regain the sand. He opens his mouth. The water tastes like copper on his tongue. The waves turn to paper, fluttering and swirling about his thrashing limbs. Rising in a swift arc, the moon leaves a train of sparks across the sky. All around him and under him and now over him are waves and waves of money. Coins fall across the surface of the lake. The wind whips the waves into tornadoes of green paper, flashing with metal disks. He feels his body being dragged under, and he lurches awake.

Steam rolls off the long grass outside the car as the sun rises in the clear sky. Isabelle stretches her arms and presses her fingers against the felt ceiling. She rubs her eyes, then braids her damp hair with deft fingers.

"Swimming!"

"After you go swimming you will drive us directly home?"

"Yes."

"Good."

"Hush."

A woman treads through the shallow surf with a sleeping baby held against her chest. A small white plane sends a narrow shadow over the surface of the water. Fishing boats dawdle in selected shoals. Isabelle strips and stands naked in the sunlight, stretching.

Guy turns his head away and squeezes his eyes shut.

"Don't be such a prude," she says. "I'm boiling hot from sleeping in the car. The air is so soft and it cools my skin."

Deep creases made across her skin by the car seat gradually smooth as she swims toward the center of the lake. Stones give way to reeds and the reeds slope away with the lake bottom. Treading water, she looks back at Guy, hunkering miserable in the shade. She watches him slap his own face.

"Come out of the shade!" she calls. "The bugs stay away from the sun." But her voice doesn't reach him.

She dives to touch the lake bed but runs out of breath before she touches anything. She kicks to the surface and gasps. Seagulls glide low, scanning for swimming fish or floating crab carcasses. A dragonfly hovers uncertainly at her shoulder before zooming back to shore. Flipping onto her back she lets the water carry her. She wiggles her toes as the air tickles her breasts.

Two young men, almost boys, wander toward Guy, pockets bulging on cut-off jeans, fists full of shells and stones. Pausing a few feet away, they survey the lake.

"Look at that," one drawls in the slightly southern accent of an Ottawa Valley teenager.

"Wow, a mermaid," the other responds. The way they laugh together makes Guy grit his teeth.

"What's she doing now?"

"I don't know. I think she's tryin' to swim to the island. She'll never make it."

"She might make it there but she can't swim back. Look at her go!"

Guy stands. He steps into the sunlight and shades his eyes. His heart backflips. Isabelle has swum so far from shore that he can barely see her. Her head and shoulders bob out of the water as she strokes evenly away. The island that the young men spoke of—Guy follows her trajectory with his gaze—is at least a kilometer away. Isabelle is farther out than the peeled beer bottle labels, farther than the rowboats, farther than the sweeping shadows of clouds. What the hell is she doing, Guy wonders, she'll drown. Even if she makes it to the island she'll get lost. Without her clothes, the bugs will devour her. She'll be eaten alive by that bloody bear. She's crazy, he thinks. Every woman in that family is just insane. Shit. Martine will kill me if anything happens to her.

"Do you have a boat?" Guy calls out to the boys. "She's my daughter. I need to get her back."

A fisherman cuts the engine on his small powerboat as he drifts in and the two young men wave their arms and wade out to negotiate with him. They point and gesticulate, and the man steps out of his boat into the shallow water, leaving the craft rocking as he struggles. Guy waits as they drag the boat in, all three together. The fisherman takes out his fishing pole, his buckets of hand-sized fish and his red tackle box. Plastic bags litter the aluminum floor. One of the boys hands a bag to Guy and suggests that he cover his cast.

The little rusty engine sputters awake. And they are off, splitting the water and bouncing in the waves as they turn the boat toward the island and follow the fading vision of an errant mermaid.

Footprints mar the narrow beach before the trees. The young men haul the boat ashore, and one of them ties the boat with a long yellow rope to a peeling birch trunk. The air shimmers with heat. Eagerly they pull T-shirts, transparent from spray, over their heads and toss them beside the released handfuls of shells and stones scattered on the floor of the boat.

"How do you track a mermaid in the forest?" the tall one says.

"She's not a mermaid," Guy grumbles. Now that he is ashore he can see that the island is much like the rest of the campground, sunny and fluffy with flowering shrubs under a tent of knotty trees. And, thinking that heavy bears are unlikely to dog-paddle all this way from the mainland, he relaxes into irritation. "Mermaids aren't pests," he adds.

"My guess is she just started walking straight," says the shorter boy. "I can see her footprints over there. She probably just kept on. She won't walk quickly, the ground will hurt her feet."

"Isabelle!" Guy calls. "Isabelle! Come back! Come out of the forest. Isabelle, come on. You promised to drive me home."

The boys laugh at Guy, tottering toward the woods, calling out pathetic demands. He glances back and notes the sunburnt shins, the indolent smile of the taller boy. "Don't forget to look up," he says. "She might hide in a tree."

"Is she okay? I mean, she's not crazy or sick or anything, is she?" asks the one with the sunburnt shins.

"No, she's not sick," Guy says, "just unpredictable. She's like her mother, only more cheerful."

They wander through the fierce array of summer foliage until they reach the other side of the island, and then they turn around and wander back again. The greenery is fully defended; thorns and sticky things drag at their arms and cling to their legs. Spiny bracken cracks beneath their feet as they thrash through without a path. Guy's voice turns hoarse. The younger men grow irritable and silent. A fierce and noisy cloud of wasps trails the search party before retreating to the honeysuckle. A determined horsefly zooms in on Guy, alights, is knocked away, advances from a different angle. From every tree something shrieks in protest at their invasion. Guy begins to feel as if his foot will burst the cast. Someone's stomach gurgles. Someone sighs and snorts.

"Did you have a fight?" the taller one finally asks.

That one, Guy thinks, asks too many questions. The other one gives suggestions but otherwise stays silent. He feels a wave of preference toward the silent one.

"No. I think she's looking for a bear, or else she just doesn't want to go home so she's hiding from me."

"How old is she?"

"She's twenty."

"How old are you?"

"Thirty-eight."

"You look even younger. It must have been tough raising a kid when you were a teenager. It's no wonder she's a little wild. You must have been wild when she was growing up. Don't worry, we'll find her. She's got to be getting hungry by now. When she's hungry enough she'll put on her clothes and come home."

"I forgot her clothes."

"Well, it was kind of a figure of speech."

"I think we should split up," says the quieter, more help-ful one. "Head in three directions from this point and comb through the forest in a circular fashion until we reach the boat again. If one of us finds her, keep shouting 'I got her' and bring her back to the boat. We'll rendezvous there."

"Will she come with one of us easily? She doesn't know us," the noisy one says.

"She's not dangerous. She's just a pain in the ass."

"*I'm* a pain in the ass?"

"Isabelle?"

"I'm up here. I'm a pain in the ass. That's a real nice thing to say about your daughter. What if I went around telling peo-ple that my father was an absentee papa? I bet you wouldn't like that."

"Were you an absentee papa?" the noisy one asks.

Guy sighs with irritation and ignores him. He can see her now, perched on a high branch, her long hair dangling down around her oval face, hiding her naked torso. He unbuttons his shirt and pulls his arms out of the sleeves. He holds the shirt out to her. "Come down. We're going home."

"I'm not going yet."

"Oh, for Christ's sake! What's the matter, Isabelle? What do you want from me?"

"I want you to agree to stay longer. I want you to come to Ste-Famille with us. I want you to promise to stay or I won't come down."

"You have to come down sooner or later."

"What's in Ste-Famille?" asks noisy, sunburnt-shins.

"We might be able to shake the tree gently," quiet and helpful says. "Or I could climb up that one beside her and throw some pinecones at her."

"Why do you want me to come to Ste-Famille? I'll only screw things up. I don't belong with your mother and you, and Harry. Look, I wish I did. I wish I had stayed around the first time and been there for you. But I didn't. And now I think I'm upsetting what little balance you have. You're better off without me. I'm hopeless, Isabelle. I can't help you. I'm an impossible klutz. Isabelle, why do you want me?"

"What difference does it make?" she calls, swinging her feet gently below the branch. "I waited for you to come back. I waited all my life. I waited because I wanted to meet you. I want you to stay a little longer."

Guy looks at her swinging legs. Vines coiled around the tree trunk seem suspiciously animate to him.

"Climb down carefully. Your mother will count every scratch on you when we get home."

"Are you staying?"

"Yes. For a little while. But I won't do anything. I'll just stay out of the way."

"That's great!" she calls. She scrambles down the trunk and lands between the three men. Guy feels a miserable hot shock as he looks away from her naked skin. He glares at the two young men as he dresses her in his shirt, imagining the fancy cravings gathering in their foolish heads. His shirt hangs to her thighs, providing him with rough relief. Together they begin walking back to the boat.

"This isn't going to become your major negotiating tactic is it, climbing a tree and refusing to come down until I do whatever you want?"

"I don't know. It works. My feet hurt."

"I can piggyback you," the suddenly not so helpful and quiet one says. He bends down, and Isabelle clambers on his back. Guy thinks to argue, but he can't make himself voice the image in his head of her specific nakedness wrapped around a stranger's back. She shrieks as the boy runs with her through the trees. The other one runs after them, and Guy trails behind, listening to his angry stomach's long harangue.

Isabelle leans over the triangular prow, her face shining in the spray, fingers trailing in the waves. She tosses her head to flip her wet hair away from her eyes. Guy stares at the back of her neck exposed by the oversized collar. He worries briefly that she may burn. His own poor face is swollen with insect bites. He feels a little dizzy looking at the water.

Sunburnt-shins steers the boat and stares at Isabelle. Quiet betrayer spreads stones retrieved from the floor on the wooden bench beside him. Isabelle turns her head and smiles at them. The sun has drawn her freckles out and her face glows with an almost amorous pleasure. The fine, colorless hairs on her upper legs glint over the lightly tanned skin.

"What's that?" she asks the one who is spreading his cache of stones. She points at a stone in the shape of a screw.

"It's a turritella, not a very good one. But here, this an ammonite. You see the spiral in the center of the shell."

She takes the shell from him and examines it closely. He flushes and offers her another stone patterned with tiny broken spirals.

"I have a fossil collection at home," he mutters.

"That's neat. Have you ever found anything special?" she asks.

"I found an opalized ammonite on a beach in Wales two years ago."

"What's that?" she says as she hands back the stones.

"A giant version of the fossils I just showed you, but scaled with calcium so it has a milky white sheen, like an opal."

"Tell me about it," she murmurs.

Now I know why Martine keeps such a sharp eye on the gangly, glowing monkey, Guy thinks.

The boy is smitten. Half moony, half preening, the one that Guy had previously trusted launches into his tale.

"I was hiking along the hills and I walked down toward the shore for a break. I was sitting on a stone wall, near one of the gun pits left over from World War Two. I was going to crawl in for a nap but it was filled with broken bottles and used condoms. So I sat on the wall and looked out at the sea. After a while I started to scan the boulders on the beach, looking for a flat one I could lie down on and take a nap. Just then the sun came out, the mist started to lift, and I could see this pattern." He traces a spiral in the air. "It was so large I could see it from the top of the wall, glowing in the sun. The bluffs and the rocks around it were completely bare. Which is weird because fossils that size are never found alone. It took awhile to reach it because I had to jump along the boulders and the water was making everything slippery. But then I found it. It was something, something unreal, like a bluish constellation, like a little Milky Way. I could see the suture pattern clearly."

"The suture pattern?"

"The pattern on the outside of a shell. It's a continuous line on the shell surface where the whorls adjoin. The largest whorl is where most of the creature's soft parts are stored. Anyway, it was at least forty centimeters in diameter—a little smaller than your forearm."

She raises her forearm to conjure the size.

"It had a violet ghosting effect over the axial sculpture, the ornamentation that runs over the outside aspect." He shakes his head, embarrassed. "It just lay there in the middle of this bleak, abandoned beach, like the face of someone buried in a rockslide."

When Isabelle looks at him, the full black circles of her pupils are exposed. She looks thrilled, Guy thinks.

"I saw Bono in a restaurant once," the other boy says.

After the convoluted morning, the shady campsite seems idyllic. The fire has collapsed into silky ash. Isabelle makes sandwiches. The two boys offer to pack the tent and the tarp and the cooler into the trunk. While they pack, Guy nurses his foot, rubbing ice from the cooler over his exposed toes and the space at the knee where the cast leans away from his skin.

"Are you all right?" Isabelle hands him a sandwich.

"My leg hurts. It feels swollen."

"I'm sorry. I have some aspirin in the car."

"It may cut my risk of having a heart attack the next time you do something crazy, but I don't think it will help the swelling. We didn't call your mother. She's going to be mad when we get home."

A crow shrieks and something scampers behind them. Isabelle looks up at the sky. She bites her knuckles and frowns. The dreary sky is purpling with rain clouds.

"The weather turns on you so quickly here," Guy says.

"Let's go," Isabelle says, her voice gone hard.

"What's the problem?" one of the boys asks.

"I'm eating my sandwich," Guy complains.

"Eat it in the car. We have to go. I can't believe I forgot to call. Why did I do that?"

"We can call at the pay phone at the park entrance."

"Fine, but let's do it right now. Let's just go, please, Guy."

"Okay, okay, we'll go. Don't yell at me. Guys, you can just throw everything in the back, we'll sort it out later."

Isabelle passes the remaining food to the young men. She leaves them the firewood and thanks them for their help. She climbs into the driver's seat and waits for Guy.

"Is it so bad?" he asks after attaching his seat belt. "Will Martine be that upset?"

She turns the key and starts the car.

At the entrance to the park they stop at the public phone, but the metal box is empty, the phone has been removed.

The journey home along the highway is elongated by silence. The radio cannot catch a station. Guy examines the heel of his hand, which feels bruised from leaning on his walking stick, tramping through the forest. As he stares at his hand it occurs to him that what is most disturbing about the sound of the radio static is the way that it perfectly echoes his own irritation. Isabelle grips the steering wheel and stares, barely blinking at the road ahead. He wonders at her sudden intensity. How mad can Martine be? he thinks. She asked us to go away. It serves her right that we forgot to call. Nevertheless, Isabelle's tension is contagious. He leans his head back and closes his eyes and hums to drown the emotional noise in his head as they head toward Ravel.

"Slow down," he mumbles. "Stop trying to kill me."

"There's a store," she says and points. "I'm going to use their phone."

At the side of the road Guy sees a small white house. It sits alone in an otherwise empty field as if it has fallen there. A plastic Pepsi sign lies in the middle of the gravel driveway.

When they walk through the door a buzzer sounds. The buzzing drops off as the door closes behind them. The long room is divided by dusty metal shelves stocked with dusty boxes of detergent, cat food, cereal and other groceries. Off to the side, beside a small counter, stands a rack of outdated magazines bearing glossy cover photos of people who were extremely famous only a few years ago. A black rotary phone sits on the counter. Behind the counter is a closed door.

"Hello," Guy calls. "Hello!"

Isabelle shushes him. She walks to the phone and lifts the receiver to her ear and then hangs it up again. "There's no dial tone."

Guy hobbles over to the door. "Allo," he calls. He pushes the door open a crack. He hears only silence from the room beyond. A warm wave of cinnamon-scented air washes past him.

"What's that smell?" Isabelle says behind him. She pushes the door open. The room in the back is a kitchen. The floors are tiled black and white, and the cupboards are painted antique blue. A long counter down the center of the room is lined with wire racks weighed down with two rows of fragrant latticed pies.

Isabelle holds a hand just over one of the golden disks. "Peach," she says. "They're still warm. I wonder where the people went."

"Would you like one of those pies?"

They look around for the owner of the high voice.

"Would you like one of those pies?" they hear someone say again.

"Yes," Isabelle calls back. "Where are you? We need to use a phone. It's an emergency."

From a door hidden behind a rolling cupboard, a little girl of about eight emerges. She stands before them in a tiny Bonjour Kitty T-shirt and rolled-up jeans. She has a round, smiling face surrounded by red curls.

"I was listening to you downstairs. I'm here by myself." She giggles. "The phone doesn't work downstairs. Would you like a pie? I can sell you a pie because I made them. I can't sell anything else—I don't know what anything costs. Would your husband like some pie?" The buzzer goes off in the store. "That's my dad."

"Lise," a man calls.

"I'm in the kitchen!"

The man stills in the doorway when he sees Guy. He is about Guy's age and build, in a blue-and-white-checked work shirt. He is unshaven, and red curls identical in hue to his daughter's tumble out from under a blue hat.

"I told you to stay downstairs," he hisses at his daughter. "Just ignore people if they come in."

"They want pie," she answers.

"We need to use the phone," Isabelle explains.

"Our phone is broken," the little girl says.

"Lise," her father snaps, "go back downstairs. I told you never to talk to strangers."

"Everybody's a stranger who comes in here," she says.

He takes off his hat and makes an effort to lower his voice. He looks at Guy. "My wife," he starts, glancing at Isabelle, "died of cancer last month. I lost my job. I told Lise she could bake some pies because I don't have gas to take her to school. She gets bored in the store all day. Go downstairs, Lise," he pleads, but the girl doesn't budge. Sighing, he turns to Guy. "I hate to ask you this," he says, "but could you please give me your wallets?"

"Daddy!"

"We just wanted the phone," Guy stutters. "I'm sorry about your family."

The man's eyes glitter with wetness. He grinds his teeth, then swallows. His hands shake. "We're eating off the shelves," he mutters between his teeth. "I can tell by looking at you, I can tell by looking at your wife, that you have some money. I'm not a thief. I am not usually a bad man. Just give me your wallets." He cranks his head and then stares at his feet.

Guy notices for the first time that the man's knuckles are skinned, brown with dried blood. He looks at the little girl. She stares at her father, clenching and unclenching small fists against her sides.

"Just give me your wallets." He shakes his head, exasperated. "I just want you to give me your wallets. I don't want to take them from you."

"Daddy." The girl's voice is thin with dread.

"Christ!" he yells. "One day you two will have kids. And all your money will drain away. One day you'll open your eyes and everything in you will scream, 'Blow your head off!' But you can't because the little leech hasn't got anybody else in the world to feed on. So you'll get up and you'll try again to get a job, to score some cash, to buy her bloody asthma inhalers and allergy medicine. And you'll hate yourself for wondering what it might be like if you didn't have her, what it might be like if you just went out and stayed out and when you came back she was gone." He makes a short miserable sound, almost a laugh, and looks down at Lise, struck silent beside him.

"And then you'll feel so guilty," he croons, "just for imagining something happening to her, you'll fight twice as hard to put things right, but you'll be even less likely to succeed because you just look so desperate."

"We're not rich," Guy stutters.

"It doesn't matter," Isabelle says softly. "Come here, sweetheart." The girl walks over cautiously. "Is your daddy always like this?"

"No. He's usually nice." Tears gloss her cheeks.

"Okay. I'm going to give you all my money for your pies. That way it's not robbery. They look like really good pies and I bet they're worth even more than I'm going to pay. I'll give you two hundred dollars. You stand here between us. Your daddy can put them in some bags for us and then we'll go. I'm sorry, I'm really sorry about your mother."

"Thank you," her father whispers. He moves to the

counter and begins bagging the pies. The intense trembling of his hands protracts every motion.

Guy and Isabelle walk to the car with six bags of pies between them. Guy looks up at the glowering sun. He gulps deep breaths to quell the embarrassment creeping up his throat. Isabelle starts the car in silence and turns back onto the road.

After a few minutes he says, "We should call the police."

"Why? To share the pies?"

"Because they robbed us."

She snorts in exasperation. "They didn't rob us. He asked for our wallets and I offered him money in exchange for some baked goods. That's not a crime. Didn't you hear him? They were hungry."

"They had a counter full of pies."

"Thank you, Marie Antoinette."

"I'm just saying that it's not your job to save the world. It's not your job to solve their problems."

"I wasn't trying to save the world, I was trying to save you. I gave them enough money to buy some groceries."

"Was the money you gave them real?"

"Yes, it was Canadian money."

"You should have offered to pay two hundred dollars for one pie and left the other pies behind so they could sell them. At two hundred dollars a pie, if they sold them all they could cover their expenses for a month."

Isabelle scowls. "Fine. What would you have done, if you were going to do anything?"

RAVEL

Guy's mind wanders as they drive. He imagines or remembers Martine holding his entire body curled against her as he cried over some childhood tragedy that he can't drag back to the present. He swallows, recalling the sensation of Martine's careful hands stroking his cheeks, wiping away his warm tears, feeding him sweet pieces of ridged licorice. He remembers the heat of her skin emanating through her clothes, and the room around them smelling of fresh paint and cut daisies. He tries to look around the room in his mind to see where they were. The kitchen in his mother's house was painted one summer, though it rained every day for a week after it was painted, and the walls just wouldn't dry. His mother loved daisies. She grew them in the backyard but never brought them inside because the little green bugs that crawled around the yellow disks made her cry out with squeamishness.

Anxiety ricochets around the hard silence of his skull.

Curtains are drawn tight behind every window except the window to Martine's bedroom. The car rolls into the driveway. Isabelle gets out without turning off the engine. Guy reaches over to turn the key.

As the front door swings open he sees Harry standing there, blinking.

"Is everything okay, Harry?" Isabelle asks.

"You didn't call," Harry says. "She cut herself."

Guy feels his skin grow cold as he looks back and forth between them.

"She's upstairs resting. The doctor says she's almost ready to be a surgeon; she followed the vein like a spelunker."

Isabelle's steps thunder over the ancient stair boards, shaking the floor. Harry turns back to Guy. His face is almost colorless, his ivory skin marred by shadows carved beneath swollen eyelids that drift open and closed over bleary eyes.

"I found her hiding in her closet," he says after a minute. "She was lying on the sheets and she had wrapped her arms in pillowcases that were dripping. I called the ambulance and I carried her down the road to be as near as possible when it drove in."

Guy starts to walk toward the stairs but Harry grabs his arm. "Leave them alone. It's Isabelle she needs."

"I'm sorry. I didn't know it was so important we call."

"Isabelle should have known. I guess she didn't."

"She's never been away from Martine before?"

Harry shrugs. Guy shifts his weight between his feet. He reaches behind his back to press the door until he hears a click. He looks at the top of the staircase.

In the bedroom doorway Isabelle pauses. Long bandages are wrapped around Martine's fists and wrists. Lying on her side, she faces the open window. The room is humid. In spite of the thick summer heat, Harry has turned on the furnace and wrapped Martine in blankets. Air from the open window carves a cool tunnel through the stifling atmosphere, and Isabelle inhales the leaf-drenched scent of the outside world. As she shifts her feet the floorboards betray her. Martine rolls over and smiles. Her face glistens with sweat.

"Hello, Beauty," she whispers. "Have you come to save the Beast?"

"Mom," Isabelle gasps. "Mom, I'm sorry."

"Hush, come here."

For minutes that stretch on and on they lie together, Martine rocking and shushing her daughter through miserable convulsions on the bed.

It seems to Guy as if the hours contract into the narrow space between his eyelids and time is squeezed into shorter and shorter increments by each blink. The night slowly encroaches. By ten o'clock the lamplight is sufficient only to describe the darkness. Isabelle stays upstairs, ashen with guilt as her mother strokes her hair with a bandaged hand, whispering something soft, unintelligible, soothing. Harry and Guy sit silently in the living room, across from each other. The clock in the hall ticks off the passing minutes.

At some point Guy begins to feel that he should say something to Harry and so he looks at him and tries to think of something kind to say.

"Stop staring at me," Harry says.

"I'm sorry. I was thinking."

"Well, think faster. You've been looking at me for five minutes."

"Sorry. Do you want to hear what happened on our trip?"

"Only if you end the story by saying, 'and that's when I realized that I had to go back to Boston.'"

Guy nods. "I'm not going back to Boston. I'm coming to Ste-Famille. Isabelle told me everything and she asked me to come. I promise I won't get in the way. I don't want to be involved. I'll just come with you and not do anything."

"Ste-Famille, Guy, fuck, *why*? Why do you think we're going to Ste-Famille?" Harry hisses.

"Isabelle told me everything," Guy repeats.

"What did Isabelle tell you? What the hell did she tell you? Doesn't what happened here tonight show you that you should leave? Everything is fucked since you got here. You're ruining everything. You'll get us all killed if you come to Ste-Famille. Why, why did you have to come back?"

"I came back to meet my daughter."

"You're a liar. I know you're a liar. If you're not a liar then you're a fool. You came back for Martine. You can't come to Ste-Famille. You can't stay here. This has nothing to do with you. I can't believe how self-important you are. Twenty years ago you ran away. You haven't done anything for these women. I've been here for five years doing everything for them. But ever since you turned up every conversation has been split in half by the question of what you want. What will Guy do? Why is Guy here? Is it good or bad that he came back? We have a million things to do and now Martine is lying upstairs sewn back together like a cloth doll and you still don't understand. *We don't need you.* Isabelle is just being romantic about having her father around. Don't you see, Guy? She grew up without you. She doesn't need you. *We* don't need you. We need our privacy."

Guy clears his throat and studies Harry's bare feet. One big toenail is black. He stares at Harry's feet as if he is trying to read his own future there. Not the future where he returns to Boston, or where he finally stays, but the future where he lifts his head and musters something kind to say to Harry.

"You saved Martine's life."

"No, I didn't. I only stalled her."

"How many times do I have to say I'm sorry?"

"How many times until it changes things?"

"We were only gone a few days. How often does she do this?"

A little bell in the square wooden clock in the hallway trills. The ceiling creaks as someone moves upstairs. An owl's voice throbs through the curtains. It sounds to Guy like the voice of a dove glutted on cream.

"It's funny," Guy says, "the things that drift through your mind when you can't think." He swallows, and the volume of the sound startles him. "She told me that she stabbed herself in the stomach once. She told me that before we left. I never should have agreed to go away. I love her, Harry. I've loved her all my life."

"You don't even know her. She's a fucking pain." Harry clucks his tongue, dismissive. "She's controlling and too smart.

She doesn't love anybody but Isabelle and she practically crushes Isabelle with love. She can't understand the connection between her own life and the lives of people around her. She had to know that Isabelle would never get over it if her mother killed herself because she didn't get a phone call. What kind of mother would do that? I'll tell you what kind. The kind that's lying upstairs in the bed, beside a laundry basket filled with bloody pillowcases."

"Stop it. I know you're angry but stop trying to force me to fight with you."

"Do you think she wants your love? Do you think she wants more people in her life? She can't stand it. She stabbed herself after Sally died. That's what she told you about. Isabelle went down in the morning to make pancakes and found Martine on the kitchen floor with a knife in her stomach. Isabelle pulled all the paper towels from the rack trying to stop the bleeding. She cried so loud that I woke up and came down and called the ambulance. I would do absolutely anything to keep Martine alive. I would even put up with you. But I think that if you stay it will be impossible. You remind her too much of her childhood. She needs to feel that this house is finally inviolable. She needs us, and only us, to be with her so that she can fight the sucking black hole that she sees when she looks into herself."

"We don't have to hate each other, Harry."

"I hate you. You do what you want."

The sound of a toilet flushing upstairs distracts Guy. He feels suddenly too weak to argue. He stands and decides to go up to his room and try to sleep. In the hallway he notices that the mirror faces the window. He looks over the reflection of his shoulder at the reflection of the room behind him. It's not enough, he thinks. Between the mirror and the window is me. Between my insides and the outside there's nothing but my skin. It's just not enough, my skin, to protect the world from me, or to protect me from the world.

———————

"Shh, don't move. Everyone is asleep," Martine whispers.

The mattress dips as she leans on Guy's bed. Dense darkness floods his open eyes. With the blinds pulled and the thick curtains drawn over them, not even the shadows are visible.

"Martine? I can't see you."

"Do you remember when you were little, you stayed overnight when our mothers were playing cards?"

"Yes."

"We slept in the same bed together, head to foot. Halfway through the night you'd go to the bathroom and when you came back you'd crawl in beside me and put your head on my pillow and we cuddled until morning? Hold me like I used to hold you. I feel scared."

"Okay." He lifts the covers. He hears footsteps pad around the bed and then she slides in beside him. His left arm has fallen asleep and he must move it, meat-like, out of the way to make room for her. With a slight shock he realizes that she is naked except for the bandages. Her skin is feverishly hot beneath a film of sweat. She lies against him and his instant erection nudges her legs.

"My arm is asleep."

The smell of Martine's hair is clouded by an unfamiliar hint of illness. Guy moves his hand and arm to activate his muddied nerves. His fingers tingle painfully.

"Lie still," she says.

"Martine, why did you do it?"

"Don't ask me that, Guy. There is no why."

"I want to understand you, but—"

"You don't want to understand me. You want to change me. Do you want to fuck?"

"No. I really don't think I could bear it. Is that your answer to everything?"

"It's not meant as an answer."

He hears her swallow repeatedly and he feels her fingers squeezing and clinging to his shoulder. "Don't cry, please. I hate it. Don't cry. I'm right here."

"I can hear the stars screaming," she mutters.

He pats her back and turns his head to touch his mouth against her hair. "It's not the stars screaming," he says, "it's just your nervous system. Think about your heartbeat. That will calm you down."

"I'll listen for your heart instead. Move your shoulder. There, I can hear it. Your heart sounds like my mother chopping radishes."

Martine slips one hand under the sheets and touches Guy's erect penis. She encircles the head with her thumb and forefinger. She moves the circle of her fingers down the shaft as if she is pushing and withdrawing a ring along a finger. A bead of sperm escapes and wets the web between her forefinger and her thumb.

He moves his hand, a wide-awake hand, over her body. He touches her nipple with the tip of one finger. He licks his fingertip and traces the areola.

After a minute he reaches down and finds her knee. The rough texture of her knobbly knee reassures him. Everything will be all right if she still has rough knees. Her bony toes scrape his calves as she straddles his hips. She leans over and kisses him as he squeezes her narrow nates. No sound interrupts her movements.

The air in the room, is it from potpourri in the drawers? The air smells of crushed flowers. He feels an itching desire to penetrate his own skin with the strength of his arousal. He pictures his cock glowing so brightly inside of Martine that he might be able to see himself between her hip bones. He imagines a rose glow filling the room. Illuminated, her body filling with the fire of ejaculate. He kisses her again. The bottoms of his feet itch. A sensation glowing in his groin flares, and the pressure to push, to piss, to gasp is too great. He comes.

Martine slips off his body. A link of come breaks as they part. He draws deep breaths of fresh air down to the bottom of his lungs. She falls onto his outstretched arm and rests.

When he opens his eyes again the morning sun is flaring off the white sheets. The curtains are open and the blinds are up.

Martine lies curled on the floor in front of the cupboard, mummified hands folded beneath her head. He raises himself up in bed to look at her. With her knees drawn up to her chest and her hair fallen over her face she looks, for the first time, like the gentle young woman that he remembers. His throat tightens. He moves his legs over the side of the bed and stands up quietly. His cast thumps against the floor. He draws the coverlet off the bed. She does not wake. He covers her and, leaning against the closed closet door for leverage, he lifts her sleeping body and carries her, awkwardly, two steps to the bed. She rolls out of the coverlet into the sheets.

"Martine," he says softly, sitting beside her on the bed. He strokes her bandages. She sleeps on with her mouth open. "I'm such a fool. I look at you and I become so foolish. You make us all fools, me, Harry, Isabelle. We all hang on to you like some golden goose. Only you're a crazy goose, and we all go crazy being dragged along behind you."

Listless and stunned, Isabelle sits in a stained-pine swivel chair at a tiered desk in the basement; her face is lit by the awful glow from a computer screen. She stares at the screen, leaning in, seeing nothing, working her lower lip between her teeth. She wears only a rumpled gray T-shirt and modest cotton panties. Her disheveled hair is drawn back in a loose ponytail. Her hand, cupping the mouse on the pad, is completely still.

"So this is it," says Guy.

Isabelle spins in her chair to observe her father on the open staircase. He reaches up to pull a string connected to a short chain dangling beneath a bare lightbulb. The light turns on with a click. As he walks through the room toward her he tugs at more strings and the bulbs luminesce. He stops in the middle of the room to survey the contents collected beneath the homely low ceiling. He turns on his heel, seeing a machine, white and large, which looks like a photo-developer from a one-hour photomat. The words on the side of the machine are in an Asian script. Beside the machine is a long plywood table with metal legs pushed up against a wall. By the furnace, a giant dehumidifier chirrs steadily. Scattered in the corners of the room are stacks of stretchers—wooden frames with nylon mesh stapled taut across them. A trough of mulch. A long box that looks like it might contain skis.

Isabelle sits in front of a silver-colored flat computer screen; an ordinary laser printer sits on one side of her, a scanner on the other. Over the desk, on a rough corkboard, American bills of several denominations are pinned in overlapping sheets.

"It's almost five o'clock," he says. "I think it's time to put some pants on. Hey? I came to see if you were okay. Are you okay? Are you hungry?"

She lifts and drops her hands, palms up. She stands, and her thin brown arms beneath the terrycloth cap sleeves fall loosely against her sides. He sees a brief flash of pink fabric beneath the long shirt and it provokes in him an odd swallow of tenderness. Her long legs turn in at the knee. Her whole expression is weighted with sadness.

"Did you know she would do something like this?"

Isabelle shakes her head, but then she says, "I must have."

"She's okay now," he says. "She's been up and down sleeping but she's been up now for a couple of hours and she seems more solid. She says she won't try to kill herself again."

"Yes, that's what she says. I know I told you that you had to stay, Guy. But if she says that you can't, then you have to go."

"Is this where you make all the money?" He waves an unsteady hand to indicate the machinery.

She nods and smiles weakly. "I can show you how, if you like. I can give you a proper tour. Would you like that?"

"When Sally started, the money was simple to make, she only had to bleach out small bills and print them with the faces of higher denominations. Jules and Jim, the friends of your dad, and Mom's dad, that Sally went to for help, found someone who told her how to do it and then they set her up. The key to making money was to make a perfect negative. You had to etch an engraving on steel. You couldn't remove any mark you made, so what you did had to be perfect. There was something truly surreptitious, even erotic about the stillness required, the tiny, tiny movements and the determination you needed to make a perfect etching.

"Later, a negative could be shot with the copyboard of a camera. If it didn't work out you could just put it in a tray of Clorox, watch it all bleach out until the piece of film was clear. Of course the lovely thing about that was that you had erased your crime. None of the equipment or materials are illegal. It's only the graven image that you're never supposed to reproduce. Back then, when I was little, we had a machine the size of a pilot whale to print the bills. It was from De La Rue Giori, the same company in Switzerland that makes the printers for the Federal Reserve. But now virtually all the work can be done with this." She waves toward the computer.

Guy screws his lips up to hide a twitch. He feels a sense of awe mingling with nausea at his daughter's confident mastery. "You sound like a tour guide," he says.

"And with this." She points to the white machine. "This is a printer from Japan. It gives a high enough resolution to allow for microprinting. The newer portraits on the notes are enlarged and have been moved off-center to accommodate a watermark of the portrait embedded in the paper." She hands him a bill. "Can you see it? In that blank space to the right, yeah, hold it up to the light."

He does as she asks, holding the bill up until the ghost of Ben Franklin appears beside his portrait.

"Very nice," he says quietly and hands it back to her.

"Watermarks are no big deal to make, it's just an image made of wire that sits on the stretcher. The wire keeps the mulch from adhering as thickly to that area and so the thinness of the paper creates the image when the light falls through. But you have to get the details right. Here, look, you see the watermark is on the right side of the fifty, but it's on the left side of the hundred-dollar bill. And here, this is a polymer thread, see? It's in a different position on each bill and it reads, well, in this case, 'USA $50' when it's held under an ultraviolet light. Making thread like this is a pain but it can be done. We don't have to do it because the people we deal with give us a spool with their new order every year when we drop off the . . . Do you want to sit down?"

Guy swallows loudly.

"So, anyway, you have to embed the thread properly, close enough to the surface of the paper to be seen under the right lighting, and turning the right color red. But not so close that it's noticeable to the naked eye when it falls flat in your hand. Things like the watermark, the thread, these all prevent counterfeiting by eliminating the counterfeiters who just bleach and reprint. Doesn't do a thing to stop counterfeiting in Eastern Europe or in North Korea, where they just keep printing the old style of bill. But the U.S. ignores those bills. Partly because the countries where they're made are already in such a mess it's not worth it. And partly because as long as the money stays there, the Federal Reserve considers it 'public money.' It's made by and for the public, and staying in circulation inside the countries of origin. Another thing the Americans don't mind about international counterfeiting is that for some reason counterfeiting encourages the circulation of second-hand American goods in black markets abroad. Free advertising for democracy."

Guy clears his throat. "I'm not sure how much Levi's and T-shirts and CDs have to do with advertising democracy."

"Well, sometimes it's computers and radios and books. Russia and North Korea are the world's largest distributors of counterfeit American money, but Iran and Syria are the only countries that are actively trying to undermine the U.S. economy by printing massive amounts of U.S. dollars. The Federal Reserve calls those notes supernotes."

"Isabelle," he says, "you should at least try to mask your admiration. These are serious criminal acts."

"It was always supposed to be the world's most international currency."

"I get that."

"Anyway, things like the microprinting and—you see the concentric lines on the obverse and reverse of the bill? These blur into a solid pattern when you photocopy them, so there's another batch of amateurs eliminated. But none of these things are really difficult to overcome, you just need a really detailed, touched-up scan, an excellent printer and the proper materials. The thing that is the dead giveaway is the feel of money. People fondle their money. So it's the papermaking, which is what I do, that really gives a dollar its value."

"I always wondered," Guy says. "Why is Abraham Lincoln on the five-dollar bill? Shouldn't he be on the fifty-dollar bill instead of Grant? Lincoln is so mythic. Why put him on such a small bill?"

She gives a little laugh. "It goes by circulation. There are more five-dollar bills in circulation than any other denomination, and second to the five is the one, so you get to see those two faces, Lincoln and Washington, more often than any others. You see, even in money, numbers aren't the only indicator of value."

She rolls back and forth on her heels, softly clapping her hands against her bare upper thighs. "The newer hundreds are printed with black, white and green ink instead of just green and black ink, on very light green paper made of high-quality cotton and linen. If you print on regular paper you won't get the right colors, but you also won't get the right stiffness, that crackle and slippery raised-ink feeling of a new bill that's so scrummy in your hands. To make the paper, I cook old bills and shredded denim scraps and plain linen for several days until the fibers fall apart and lose their color. Then I drain them and wash them and cook them again. In the end I have to cook them in small batches in a pressure cooker with a bunch of very caustic chemicals. I dye the mulch that light off-white, light green color. Then I add tiny red and blue fibers shredded in the Cuisinart. I dip the stretchers, apply the security threads, dip them again, and voilà!"

"Voilà," he echoes grimly.

"Your hands are shaking. Do you feel sick? Should I stop?"

"No. I was just wondering if you have this in your genes. And if I do too."

She shakes her head and points to a large wooden frame leaning against the wall. "Well, I made these stretchers. After I dip them, I fold the paper out onto sheets of felt to drain and then press it in this." She walks over to a large metal contraption that Guy had failed to see beside the furnace. "The paper is dried and pressed in here. When I pull the lever down twenty tonnes of weight from these two plates compresses the paper and that makes it strong. Then I take the sheet and pin it with these metal arms on the table and run a round blade around the edges. Photographers trim paper with something like this. We print in the big printer and then we paint by hand a separate layer of details."

"It seems like a lot of work. Wouldn't it be easier to get a regular job in town?"

"I have no idea. We follow the details of the bill with an invisible paint pressed on with a stamp of the design. The paint raises slightly when we warm it with a hair dryer so it feel embossed. You have to have a very, very light hand for that. Harry does it. This feature is so new that people aren't used to it anyway. The treasury stamp has no black in it, and it's printed with a much heavier ink, so we apply that separately too. And then . . ." She opens the box that looks like a giant rifle case and out pops a set of metal rollers on a hidden spring. "This is an antique Dutch iron for pressing sheets. I put a bit of baby oil on the rollers. The paper goes through here. I crank it. You see the handle? That part is fun, like running a music box. This makes the paper a little more supple."

"Isabelle, why do you think you can do this?"

"Because I've tried it and I know I can do it."

"No, I mean, why do think that it's all right for you to do this?"

She sighs and shrugs as if he has asked her an unanswerable question. "This is what we do. I'm good at it, and I like it. Do you know who J.S.G. Boggs is?"

"No."

"He's an artist who makes and spends his own money. It's only images on paper, after all. It's portraiture, and landscape, it's abstract geometry. It's intaglio and embossing. It's ink on paper. There are multiple layers to building the bill, but in the end it's just something someone makes. Look at the bills on the bulletin board. Tell me if you can pick out the real money."

He steps forward on unsteady feet and studies the presidents. He sees the suggestion of a frown just beginning to pucker between Lincoln's brows; Jackson's lips look pinched as if he has just been asked to kiss someone distasteful. Franklin has an enigmatic smile, a Mona-Lisa-tender wit; he looks sympathetic. Guy notes what looks like a pair of signatures in the lower left and lower right portions of the bills: Mary Ellen Someone-or-other and Robert E. Rubin. On another bill the signature is for a Lawrence H. something. Maybe forgeries, Guy thinks. How would he know? He touches and studies all the bills but he can't be sure he sees any difference.

"They look more unhappy than they should," he says finally. "They don't look confident enough to be presidents. They look like old men made up to look romantic. Lincoln's eyes, they're too puffy. And here, on his forehead." He traces the frown lines. "He doesn't look that sad."

She leans against him, propping her chin on his shoulder. "Yes, you're right. They do look sad. They look kind of sleepy. Except for Franklin. I think he looks sympathetic. He was, after all, a printer himself. An artist named Tim Hipschen designed that portrait. He liked Franklin, I think. But these are all real. I didn't make any of these bills, except this one." She lifts a twenty-dollar bill to reveal an identical bill beneath it, but with Harry's face in place of Jackson's. "And this one." She lifts Harry's bill and shows Guy a note with no markings indicating its value but Isabelle's cheery face, young curved neck and shoulders in place of the grim mug of a dead leader.

"I can see where it must be irresistible to do that," Guy says. He turns around and moves past her. "What's that smell? It smells like sour milk."

"It's the bleach mixed with the paper to wash the ink from the bad bills. Are you okay? Are you sure you're up for this?"

"I want to know. How much do you get for the money?"

"Fifteen percent of the face value. Because we do exceptional work, it passes in the domestic market."

"Why don't you just spend it and get the whole value?"

"Because we live in Canada. And because making the money is the part we do, not distributing money. Most counterfeit money is abroad. Eighty percent of American hundred-dollar bills abroad are counterfeit. But that doesn't stop anyone from accepting them. After all, a counterfeit American dollar still buys a lot more Turkish delight than a genuine Turkish lire."

"But it's not real," he says.

"It's as real as any other hard currency, Guy. The bank's money is all virtual. Our money is public money. And it's better, cleaner than the money the bank gives you. It has no history. Our money is money that never bought slaves."

"But you said that when it leaves here, it becomes like any other money. It doesn't stay clean. You don't stay clean. And, can I ask you something? You obviously don't pay income tax. How do you pay your bills? I assume you don't have a checking account because if you did the government would have come after you for taxes by now."

She tilts her head and smiles at him. "You're right. We're in a cash business in every sense. I think it's neat that you figured that out. How would you get away with it?"

"I don't want to play Imagine You're a Counterfeiter," he says, but then he thinks for a minute. They have electricity and a phone in this house. He knows that Isabelle went to high school because Harry mentioned it. There's no way that they could stay out of sight this long. "I don't know how you did it," he says finally. "I don't know how it could be done."

"The house was built by gung-ho gangsters," she says slyly, "on land that my father was given by a dummy company from Montréal that still keeps the registration and pays the property taxes. When your dad left, Sally took you and your mother in, and then helped Belle get set up. So Belle paid our gas bill for a few years. Out of the cash Sally got for selling counterfeit money she helped people, she helped them get away, or she helped them get back on their feet. Sometimes she helped them with their medical bills. So when Belle moved to Boston, the gas bill started going to a librarian in Estérel. The bartender's wife pays the phone bill. A principal at a high school in Toronto pays the electricity. I went to school for a couple of years but I was never registered. A lot of things around here were gifts. The flowerbeds in the garden, and the lawn, come from a woman who owns a nursery in North Hatley. So that's how we stay invisible. Pretty much all the information that there is about our existence is scattered across a wide radius. People help us to erase our steps because when they needed help, any kind of help, Sally helped them."

"What's a dummy company?" Guy asks weakly. His vision is whitewashed briefly by a lack of oxygen.

"Let's not talk about this anymore," she says, reaching for his wrist and checking his pulse. "You look like you're going to faint. Maybe I should show you some pictures of me as a kid instead."

MONTRÉAL

It is six o'clock and the sky is bright. On one side of the broad street is a bank of expensive restaurants. The customers grouped around tables and the waiters in their expensive clothing are displayed in the bay windows on the third, second and first levels of each Victorian building. Large, lazy bouncers guard the stairwells at the base of each building. They turn away flushed underage boys and extort money from pretty underage girls at the entrances to the bars. The opposing bank of buildings seems to lean into the street with garish pink and blue and green fluorescent signs that promise forty shows a night, cages of girls, girls on girls, every kind of girl, and steak dinners half price with a girl. Two young men, one with a face riddled with pimples, and the other nondescript, enter the club that advertises the cheapest dances in Montréal, eight dollars a lap dance. There is a New Year's Eve theme here every Sunday, no cover charge, and five-dollar liquor shots, but a minimum of three drinks is required and a maximum of two hours can expire before you must drink more.

"Cocoa," one of the men yells in the ear of the waitress when she bends to take his order. She shakes her head and purses her lips.

"You don't have cocoa?"

She shrugs.

"You have it or don't you?" he yells.

She looks around. "I can bring you one after you have three drinks," she says finally. "Nobody drinks three cocoas."

"That's stupid. Bring me a Canadian Club and ginger ale."

She nods. "Do you want a dance with that?" she asks.

"For fuck sake." He laughs. "Yeah, give me a CC and ginger and that one, over there." He points to a Chinese girl in a silver bikini leaning over the front of the stage, displaying her smooth buttocks to another customer.

"An Export," the man's companion says when she looks his way. "I don't need a dance yet."

She moves off. The Chinese girl turns from the stage and rolls her body, arms in the air, almost in time to the loud, distorted music.

"There's a room in the basement with beds," the man who ordered cocoa yells and points at the floor with his index finger. "You can take a girl down there and fuck her for thirty dollars. If you can't get a clean bed you only pay twenty. But if you ask them not to change the sheets they charge you forty." He laughs and coughs as he lights a cigarette. He yawns, stretching his arms and then linking his hands behind his head. There are fifteen or twenty girls planted evenly around the room. Linked foil letters spelling "Happy New Year!" are strung over the bar. The stage is dark, except for a low yellow light shining on the brass rail that pierces the room. So they must be trying to push the lap dances before the next set of strippers traipses out, elevated on clear acrylic heels that shine blue under the black lights.

"At midnight," he starts to speak again, "the girls take off their tops, the ones that are still wearin' 'em, and throw confetti, and yell 'Happy New Year!'" He waves his hands and makes a face. "You can get two lap dances for the price of one until one o'clock."

"It's a long time to midnight. Can we talk business?"

"Sure. Yeah, sure. Okay, you took too long," he says to the Chinese girl who has arrived at his elbow with the waitress. "I don't want you anymore." She and the waitress exchange looks and the girl waves at him and moves away.

"There's too much ice in the glass," he says. "I want a drink, not a freezie."

"The ice cuts down the amount of mix, Axel," his friend says. "If you have less ice, the drink is weaker. Pay her."

"I wanted cocoa," Axel grumbles, but he pulls out a five-dollar bill and five quarters and drops them on her tray.

"Here, take this," the other man says, handing her a twenty. "And pay the girl we sent away. Sorry."

She smiles and hesitates, possibly thinking of what to offer next, but then she looks again at the vivid acne on the face and neck of the man who wants cocoa and she leaves them.

"You're lucky Jim didn't kill you when he caught you following him," Axel's companion begins solemnly. "Why'd you let him catch you?"

"Don't worry. I played it like I wanted to meet him. Like I was looking for a date."

The other man snorts quietly and sips his beer. The DJ announces a new round of dancers in a rolling voice. The music rises and a spotlight hits the mirrored back wall. A slender blonde strides on stage wearing black stockings beneath an untucked police shirt, complete with badge and tie. In no time the shirt and the tie are removed and only the hat and the stockings remain. She braces her hands against the mirrors, filthy with palm prints, as she dances.

"Let's go over the plan."

"Okay. This rye-and-ginger sucks. What do you want me to do?"

"I don't want you to do anything until we're in the hotel with them. He's seen you. Do you think he'll remember you?"

Axel frowns. His eyes are back on the Chinese girl, who is naked now, straddling another man's lap.

"Are you paying attention? We can't fuck this up, Axel. Hey, look over here. These old guys are killers. If we want to take their money we need to plan, carefully."

"Yeah, I know. Can't I look at a woman while I listen to you? Get over yourself. I will stay away from Jim and Jules until we get them at the hotel. How much do we have to give the desk clerk for calling us?"

"Five grand."

"How do you know you can trust him?"

"I plan to scare him before I pay him."

"So we get the money. We pay the thumbless desk clerk." Axel laughs. "And we split the rest and I don't have to listen to your anal plans anymore?"

"Yeah, that's right, Axel. You don't have to listen to my bullshit anymore."

"I'm joking, man. Jeez, you're a sensitive fucker. Can I get a dance now?"

"If you have a dance will that get you off enough that you can listen to me?"

"Yeah."

"Okay."

Axel stands up and motions to a brunette and blonde standing together at the bar. They whisper together and then walk over, unsmiling. The brunette has small breasts, cupped tightly in a white bra. The strings of her matching lace thong rise over the waistband of a dark red leather miniskirt. The blonde has big breasts, generously fake. Her outfit consists of a transparent green sheath dress. Her dark nipples are clearly visible, as is the black V of her bikini bottom.

"I want you to dance together," Axel commands, sitting down and spreading his legs wide. The girls stand still, looking at each other silently until one smiles and mutters something in French. A new song begins and they each straddle one of Axel's legs and begin to roll their hips and stroke their own breasts.

At the end of the song the waitress arrives, unbidden, with another tray of drinks.

"Do you want a picture with them?" she asks.

"Sure," Axel says. "Let me light a cigarette. I look better when I'm smoking."

The two naked women, faces smudged with lipstick, pose on either side of Axel. They smile obediently for the flash of the Polaroid camera.

"Here, that's your mother, with me at the zoo."

Leather-bound photo albums are spread between them on the table. She points at the photograph. His mother, young again, clasps the chubby, raised hand of a grinning blond child in a bright green-and-white gingham dress. In the background, a camel turns a sly, long-lashed eye to the camera. Guy swallows. Isabelle turns the page, and he sees a cache of Christmas images. On the floor, the girl in the pictures joyfully emancipates large gifts from paper wrapping. She sits in front of a Christmas tree, which is ornamented with lights and popcorn strings, and holds up a doll in a wedding gown, an oversized children's dictionary, a plastic miniature Santa Claus. At the kitchen table the same girl slaps her hands on the surface and screams with laughter. In the yard, in a snow-suit, she pumps her legs on a swing set that is half-buried in the snow. Stretched by time, an older version of her delivers a speech on a stage, long hair pinned neatly in a ballerina bun above her fragile neck, index cards clutched dutifully at her waist. Suddenly she is a teenager, with an exophoric beauty, a stargazer lily pinned to the breast of her strapless floral sheath dress. She lifts the full bell of a glass of red wine to the camera and grins.

"It's a lot to absorb," he says finally.

"Look, I have a picture of you."

She reaches for another album and flips backwards until she finds a hazy snapshot of a lissome boy. He looks uncertain, hands pitched into the pockets of loose jeans. His soft face is lowered, trying to smile, flushing beneath long bangs. Branches from the old apple tree edge into the picture, white blossoms frilling the frame.

"You must have been around sixteen when that picture was taken."

He nods. He doesn't remember the day; it could have been any one of many.

"Okay, we'll put that away now. Do you want to see more pictures?" She opens another album.

"Look," she says. She pushes the pages toward him. "This is where you would go." She points to a space behind Martine in the living room. In the picture, Isabelle sits on the floor deeply absorbed in drawing. She points to similar blank spaces in other images. "And here, here, here you are."

"But I wasn't there. You can see that."

"You're not looking. Don't look for where you are. Look for the space where you aren't, and then picture yourself there."

He shakes his head; all he can see is the mounting evidence of his absence.

Hours later she ascends from the basement. He stands at the kitchen counter, making a late-night omelette, breaking eggs on the edge of a stainless steel bowl and cupping the yolks in the broken shells. He slips the egg whites into another bowl and turns back to the counter. She settles in a chair at the kitchen table and watches him shred cheddar cheese and slice mushrooms. He adds milk to the egg whites and whips the two together. Butter melts in a pan on the stove.

"Do you want an omelette?" he asks softly.

"No. I have something for you." She slips a manila envelope onto the table. "I'm going up to bed," she says. By the time he turns around she is already gone.

On the covers of the made bed in his room he rolls on his side and reaches beneath the lampshade to click on the shallow light. He fumbles with the unsealed envelope, releasing a set of photographs onto the covers. He moves the pictures around without picking them up, turning over the few that fell face down. He feels a pinching between his eyes. Isabelle has PhotoShopped old pictures, inserting his own impossibly insecure self into the images of her first homecoming. There he is, in front of the house, between his mother and Martine. Sally must be behind the camera. His outfit of jeans and a T-shirt is incongruous against the snowy landscape. Baby Isabelle's tiny face is barely visible, a sleeping pink oval in a cocoon of wraps.

He knocks quietly on her door, touches the wood with his flat hand and it falls open. She is awake, sitting up against the pillows, reading a book.

"I looked at your present," he mutters from the doorway. "It was sweet of you. But I still wasn't there."

She folds the book closed and places it on the night table. Gathering her knees, beneath the sheets, in her arms, she says, "Yes, you were. Use your imagination. Try and remember. You were very nervous. Mom went into labor while she was mixing ink in the basement. Sally called your house, and you and your mother drove Mom to the hospital, moaning in the backseat, her sweating face in Sally's lap. At the hospital you played cards with a winemaker from Montérégie in the waiting room. People still thought birthing was a women-only event. So Sally held one of my mother's hands and your mother held the other. And you lost money steadily, because you can't bluff a Québécois winemaker.

"Finally I came. The doctor held his breath because I was so small. Only five pounds, even though I was full term. Mom began to cry and laugh all at once. Her legs were slicked with blood and water. Sally came to get you and you dropped your hand of cards and walked in a trance into the scrubbing area. Your mother helped you wash your hands and arms. She kept steering your face back to the sink. She dressed you in a gown. She was so proud and lovely. When you held me your entire self shattered and then re-collected, the same but not the same, not ever again, because you knew that you would never really be alone, not with me in the world. You remember, don't you?"

"So Martine is the golden goose and we're all stuck to each other because of her."

"Harry," Isabelle says.

"What? Don't you think anything he says is stupid?"

"Don't eavesdrop. And if you do, then don't tell me about it. Just sort the money. We're really far behind."

Isabelle and Harry are at the kitchen table. Isabelle sits quietly, sorting green bills into piles of the convincing and the less convincing. Her bare toes trail the linoleum under her chair as she counts.

"I was just walking past his room. I didn't even know she was in there."

"Why didn't we do any fives this time?" Isabelle asks.

"They didn't ask for any. There's no point in doing fives, it's a lot of work."

"They're ugly, aren't they?" Isabelle picks up a twenty-dollar bill and holds it up against the light. "I mean, they're not attractive people, politicians. It's funny how watching movies has made ordinary people expect important people to look beautiful. It's almost never true. Scientists aren't beautiful, generals aren't beautiful, even the scriptwriters and directors of the very films that make us think that important people are beautiful don't have to be beautiful. Some of the more recent presidents are better looking. Why don't they put some new faces on the bills?"

"Because it's illegal to put the face of a living person on government securities. Believe it or not, those presidents are more attractive in the etchings than they ever were in person."

"Maybe, maybe not. Maybe if you were in the room with one of these men, and you knew he was the president, and he had the power to do something for you, to grant an acquittal for you, maybe he would look fantastic."

"I think he would look bloody awful. Powerful people look hideous when you're helpless."

"What if he could save your life?" Isabelle asks. She leans forward and holds up the bill so that the president is facing Harry. "What if you were a criminal?"

"I am a criminal."

"I mean a real criminal, someone who broke an important law. You know, like stealing state secrets, like the Rosenbergs."

"We do steal from the state, Isabelle," he says gently.

"We steal from the United States, if you must call it that. But we're not American. We bring money into Canada by doing this, so what we do is good for our economy. Anyway, what if you met this man and you were condemned to execution? What if you were in a room alone with him, and he could save your life, or save the life of someone you loved, wouldn't he seem beautiful?"

"No, Isabelle. And that's Andrew Jackson, by the way."

"I know it's Jackson." She pouts.

"Well, for someone who knows the faces of former American presidents in intimate detail, you make startling use of American history. If I were Julius Rosenberg in a room with Harry Truman, he would be horrifying. If he could spare my life, it would be because he owned it. It wouldn't be my life. It would be his. Every time you look at a dollar bill you are reminded that you work for the state. Your life's value is calculated by the number of hours you work and the value of the work in the economy. That value is meted out in dollars, and dollars buy more life for you. Dollars dictate the kind of produce you can buy, the kind of holidays you can or can't take, the number of children you can have and the kind of illnesses that you can survive. Every day of your life can fill a photo album with the faces of dead presidents. That's why I hate money. That's what makes it fun to make a hundred thousand useless presidents."

Harry sweeps a handful of bills onto the floor and picks up another handful of bills from the table and stuffs them into his mouth, chewing them and growling at Isabelle like a dog until she laughs. The refrigerator clicks on, and Isabelle sighs and leans over to pick up the bills that lie scattered on the floor. Harry takes the money out of his mouth and offers it to her.

She laughs. "Those are all wet and wrecked."

"They look more convincing this way."

"Well, you smooth them out. I don't want your spittle on me."

Harry leans over and licks Isabelle's cheek.

"Get away, you bad dog. Sit, sit and sort the money with me."

Harry sits down across the table from Isabelle and watches her sorting. For a few minutes the only sound is the rustling of the money and the whirring of the ancient refrigerator.

"Why does he have to stay?" Harry says. "Weren't we doing fine without him? What do you both see in him?"

She sighs and stares at Harry. She reaches out and strokes his cheek. He is still unshaven. She runs her fingers through his fine ginger-ale-colored hair. She can smell raspberry soap on his skin.

"I want him to stay, Harry. Maybe I just can't stand to watch anyone leave. I want you here too. I want us all to be a family."

"What's so great about a family, Isabelle?"

"A family . . . ," she tries, "a family is like a magic trick. Magic because it produces more people, and I guess because no matter how much it's injured, it just keeps going on in some form, even when all the odds are against it."

"You've been thinking about this."

She laughs nervously and then she smacks Harry in the chest with the flat of her hand. He grabs her wrist and pulls her off her chair to the floor. She digs her fingernails into his leg by the knee. She has one arm behind her back and the other arm flails madly to catch him as he pins her on the floor. She kicks the table leg and the neat piles of bills topple over.

"Don't kiss me, Harry," she says.

He lets her go. "I wasn't going to kiss you, you freak. That would turn the tables, wouldn't it? I should kiss you until your mother gets jealous."

Isabelle gives him a gentle pinch. "Please don't be hurt. Help me count the money."

On the cream grid of tiles in the bathroom lies a pile of yellow bathsheets. Martine sits on the closed lid of the toilet and Harry leans over her. Kneeling on the bath mat, he unwraps the bandages around her wrists. The stained coils wind around and hang by her legs. Harry unplugs a jar of alcohol and up-ends it, catching the clear flame in a cotton pad. He dabs the stitches and strokes the red strip of closed skin. She shifts her feet and bites her lips. Harry blows on the wound to relieve the heat. He lifts ice from a bowl on the floor and holds a frozen handful against Martine's neck, under her hair. He dresses the wounds with bright new bandages, clipping the gauze in place with metal bows.

The pale, bumpy twins of her knees tremble from the pain, and her toes curl in the furry bath mat. The bathroom mirror drips with steam from the shower. She can see the blurry colored outline of her face and shoulders reflected back above the counter.

"I'm very mad at you," she says.

Harry sits down hard on his hip and wraps his arms around her legs. He puts his head in her lap and squeezes her legs.

"Oh, Harry, fight back. I was joking. I'm not mad at you. You should be mad at me. You should be furious."

She looks down at his bent head. He strokes her leg silently. "You have to stop saving my life," she says, watching him roll his forehead against her skin. Lifting his face with a hand under his chin, she says, "You look pretty in the sunlight."

He moves his hands carefully over her thighs, giving her time to catch them. She lets her legs fall open, bracing her feet far apart on the floor. He kneels between her thighs, licking and gently suckling the little bump of her clitoris. He buries his nose in the curls of hair over her mons veneris. His tongue skims one set of labia and then the other and then enters her vagina. He kisses and kisses her as the damp of his saliva begins to pry some heat from her body.

She squeezes his ears between her thighs and winces at his earnest expression. His chin and neck grow wet. He's so young, she thinks. His skin is so seamless. His lips are very swollen. She slides to the floor and wriggles to get comfortable on the cool porcelain checkerboard. He tries to put his hand down between her open legs but she catches his fingers. Kissing his sweating neck, she opens his trousers and guides him inside her.

"Do your wrists hurt?" he asks.

"No. I feel good."

"I like these little wrinkles around your eyes and on your neck." Harry strokes her face with his fingertips.

"I look old, is that what you're saying?"

"No. No, you look gorgeous. You look refined, perfect. I like how soft and warm you feel when I'm inside you. It still feels good, doesn't it?"

"Yes. You're a very good lover."

"The last five years, since I've been with you and Isabelle, have been the best of my whole life."

She kisses his forehead. "I forget sometimes that you were just a teenager when you came to live with us. Teenage boys think so much about sex, it's hard to imagine that they think about anything else. These aren't the best years of your life. You feel experienced because twenty-two is the oldest you've ever been. But it's not very old at all. You can't let me hurt you the way I do. You can't let me be so important. You're so perfect. You're so beautiful, and kind when you want to be. You're going to find a great love, Harry. You're going to find lots of them."

He hugs her tightly. "No, I won't, not if you don't love me. I don't think I ever remember being loved. My parents must have loved me but I don't remember."

"I'm sure they loved you," she says. "I'm absolutely sure."

"I know you don't love me," Harry says. His voice takes on a cautious, experimental tone. "But whatever you feel is enough. I know it's enough, because I know what it feels like when it isn't enough."

Martine touches his closed eyelids and strokes his eyebrow with her thumb. "Ah, accounting for lovers. You must break even, though you can't break even. I spent so much time fucking you; I should have spent some of that time talking to you. It's not your fault that I don't feel romantic love. You don't have to keep straining to reach me, because I'm here, as much as I ever will be. I'm sorry. Maybe there's something wrong with me, Harry, but there have only ever been two people that I could even bear loving. I even held back from them. But there's a chemical force between mothers and daughters, it's instant and unshakable. From the first moment that I smelled my mother's skin. It's like, here I am, all alone, all of a sudden, forced into the world, screaming, and then, click, I'm in love. I know it must have been that way because that's how it was for me with Isabelle. One minute I'm shaking and empty, and utterly isolated by the pain, and the next minute, everything in the universe alters. I'm utterly alone, and then, click, I'm in love. I know you want me to say that I love you too. But, darling, sweet, wonderful boy, every other feeling that I've ever had is useless. It always falls apart."

A square wicker basket the size of a filing box sits on the maple tabletop in front of Isabelle. The basket is filled with neat stacks of bills wrapped in thin red elastic bands. The rejected bills are stuffed into a stainless steel soup tureen on the floor. Harry, Martine and Guy enter the kitchen in single file. Outside, birds squabble over space in the trees. Sunlight grazes the countertops as the day recedes.

Harry opens the refrigerator door. "We're out of beer."

"We never have beer," Isabelle answers him quietly. "Have some pie." Harry clutches his stomach and groans in response. "Can you get me a glass of milk while you're there, please?" she asks.

"Sure. I forgot, there's nothing but wine in this house. I'm going into town to get some beer. Does anybody want anything?"

"We don't have enough money," Isabelle says.

"I have money. Do you want some ice cream, Isabelle?"

"I mean there aren't enough passable bills. We're way short. There are too many smeared or uneven bills."

"Relax, Isabelle," Martine says. She takes a chair beside her and reaches into the basket. Guy watches in silence as the two women pull out stacks of notes and unwind the elastics to begin counting again.

"How much are we missing?" Harry asks.

"We're supposed to bring six hundred thousand," Isabelle says. "We're short eighty thousand dollars, give or take." She, Martine and Harry cast accusatory glances across an invisible triangle.

"Where did it all go?" Harry asks.

"It didn't go anywhere. It was ruined. Smudged, too big, too small, we always ruin some, but this is too much. It's too much!"

"All right. I'll get more pigment and ink in town. Look over the rejected bills again and see if we can pull any more out. Do we have enough pulp? Martine, is there more pulp?"

The pot of faulty bills reflects her silence. "We can tear up the rejects and unroll the cigarettes," she says finally. "I'll look to see what else we can pull together. Buy some paper, glue and linen. Take Guy with you."

Harry looks at Guy, still standing in the doorway, hands in his pockets, a short, sharp vertical line dividing his gathering brow. "I can do it by myself. He doesn't want to be involved."

"*Take* him, Harry. Do what I say. Isabelle and I will start tearing up the money."

Isabelle gathers a handful of bills from the pot and begins shredding them. Green pieces flutter from the table with the breeze created by her hand movements. "Put them in some-thing, Isabelle. You might as well soak them in the bleach solution."

Harry turns and opens a cupboard to pull out another steel pot. He deposits the pot on the table and walks briskly past Guy toward the front door.

"Go, Guy. We need to concentrate," Martine pleads.

He hears the car start outside.

As Harry steers the ancient vehicle, the car seats shudder beneath them from bumps in the road. Guy gazes ahead at the fields unfolding into the distance. Swaths of grass have fallen over in the wind. Patterns braid toward the horizon. Green hedges divide a few gold acres from the wide landscape. A brown mule contained by the hedges nuzzles the furry side of her own miniature. He watches them touching muzzles together in the shade of a tree, and then they are whisked away as the car wheels spin, carrying him forward in time.

Harry leaves Guy in the car while he stalks the tiny shops in Estérel. The shops are all in the main floors of houses along the main street. Bay windows display fruit pies, bags of almonds and chocolates, cotton dresses and straw hats, art supplies. The upper floors of the stores are curtained into privacy, and Guy imagines scruffy adolescent boys working at small desks beside single beds, configuring and reconfig-uring answers to their homework.

Harry comes out of the art supplies store and walks up to Guy's open window. "I'm going to Chantelle's for a beer. You can get out of the car now and come with me if you want."

"Who's Chantelle?"

"She was the barkeep's mother, a friend of Sally's. But now Chantelle's is the name of the bar, and the barkeep's daughter. His name is Johnny."

"Do you want a beer? I'm buying. What will you have?"

"You can order for me, Harry."

"Okay, Johnny, give me two cans of your cheapest beer."

Johnny looks skeptical. "I've got an old case of Lone Star. But the cans are dented. Let me get you something better than that." Johnny gesticulates with the wounded pride of a man being asked to do his least.

"Bring me the dustiest cans with the deepest dents and don't wash the glasses," Harry announces. "I'm treating my friend here."

Johnny wipes the counter with a towel. Meticulous, he polishes the brass bar rail as if to distract the men from the headless, rancid beer. The uneasy ceiling fan clatters overhead as it rotates. A young woman, seventeen or eighteen, in loose, low-slung jeans and a tight white T-shirt with the red Cymru dragon printed across the center sweeps the wooden floor without moving the chairs. The dust rolls like smoke in the bands of light falling through the narrow windows.

When she reaches the bar she smiles at Harry, and he offers her a sip from his beer mug. She laughs. Brown coils of her long hair are tucked behind small, flushed and freckled ears. Her tanned cheeks are rouged and her lips shine when she licks them. Harry puts a hand on her arm and pretends to test her muscle. Guy watches silently, his untouched can still perspiring on the bar beside his empty glass.

"You flirting with my daughter?" Johnny asks.

"I have only honorable intentions, Johnny. I want to see if Chantelle has the muscle to carry the twins that we're going to have and the laundry at the same time."

Chantelle laughs and pushes Harry away. "Harry has a bride already, maybe two, I've heard," she says.

"Harry has no brides," he says. "But Harry has a friend here"—he puts an arm around Guy—"who needs some pleasant company to take his mind off a leprous foot."

"I don't have leprosy," Guy says. He feels his cheeks burn. "I broke my foot."

"How did you do that, friend?" Johnny prompts.

"Martine again," Harry answers.

"Hostie, Harry. When are you going to give up on that witch? There's a world full of real women with sweet-smelling hair out there for you. I'd even let you take my Chantelle in a couple of years if you'd give her half of what you give Martine."

"Where's the fun in that, John?" Harry toasts the bar and drinks his beer.

Guy stares at Johnny. "Don't talk about her like that in front of me," he says. "I grew up with Martine. She's not a witch."

"If she's not a witch then how does she get all the young men out to the country and send them rolling back in here looking like they've been to Bosnia? Here, you don't have to drink that beer. I'll give you a fresh pint on the house. I grew up with Martine too. What's your name?"

"Guy."

"Guy? She used to have a kid who tagged after her named Guy. Is that you?"

"No. That was someone else."

Johnny leans across the bar and grabs Guy by the chin. "It looks like you. I remember you now," he says gently. "And you don't think she's a witch."

Guy twists his face away.

Johnny pours himself a beer from the tap and sips it. "When I met her I thought she was a miracle," he says. "She used to lay baby Isabelle down in the sand on the beach and strip for me. I used to hum some stupid version of a stripping song and she swung her skirt and flashed her shoulders and her tits at me. If it was raining we put Isabelle in the front seat of the car and lay down in the back with the radio tuned to the CBC. She was like a drug. I thought I couldn't go without her. I asked her to marry me. Before I met my wife and my daughter Chantelle was born, of course. My wife is the very opposite of that woman. She's kind and she's easy. Well, not when the subject of Martine comes up. That witchy bitchy witch."

Guy looks at Johnny and he sees a younger man. He sees the lanky body and rough casualness of a teenager hidden beneath the fat resignation of the adult man. He imagines for a second that he hears Johnny laughing at him. He feels a sudden spike of anger and gruffly reaches for his glass, knocking it over as he does so. He watches with shock as the golden liquid flows over the bar onto the floor.

"All right, let's go. The witch is waiting, Johnny. Sorry about the spilled beer. Here's ten extra. You know how it is, we've all been screwed by Martine. Come on, Guy, let's go."

A nerve in Johnny's cheek twitches beneath his skin. "Look at you," he sneers. "She's a whore. She's a slut. She's a polecat."

"Come around the bar and say that again," Guy spits, angry at his own embarrassment.

"I'm not going to fight a leper." Johnny waves his hand dismissively.

"I'm not a leper, you fucking shit-eating"—Guy gasps—"small-town turd!"

As if sleepwalking, he lifts his beer mug, looks at it and then throws it on the floor. The glass cracks in half and falls apart. Chantelle steps back. Her father walks around the bar. He bends over by Guy's feet and picks up the broken glass. He puts the glass on the bar and leans over again. He grabs onto Guy's cast and twists it, pulling Guy off his feet in one wrenching movement. Guy cries out as he hits the floor and kicks up with his other leg, catching Johnny in the jaw. Harry tries to step in but he slips on the wet floor and the three men are wrestling.

Chantelle yells, "Stop it, don't fight! Don't bite my dad! You're crazy. You're all crazy. Stop it! Get out! You fuckers!"

Guy has a handful of Harry's hair in one hand and a handful of Johnny's testicles in the other, he twists both and swings his cast until he catches someone in the face. Johnny digs a finger into Guy's ear and digs as if to grab him by the brain. Harry rolls over on top of them both and throws punches at random. Guy knocks over a chair and tries to swing it but only succeeds in dropping it on himself. Chantelle is behind the bar pitching ice at them until the floor is full of hail.

"Okay, okay. I'm calling Martine!" she yells. The bodies on the floor stop thrashing and three faces turn to watch her threaten them with the telephone receiver. "I will. I swear to God, I'll call her. Dad, Harry, you, leper. I'll call her and I'll call my mother and the three of you will sleep in the garbage tonight."

A martial-arts showdown between two leather-clad women in a rubber jungle floats on the bowed screen of the small television in the living room. Martine and Isabelle stand facing each other on the throw rug; the coffee table is pushed back against the couch. Giggling and glancing periodically down at the TV, they imitate the kicks and spins and punches in mock battle. Isabelle spins and punches the air in front of Martine as she calls out to Harry and Guy, "Look at me! I'm the toughest broad in the butt-kicking business!"

Martine drops her fists in shock. "What happened to you? Were you fighting each other?"

"Not specifically," Guy says.

"We were in a car accident," Harry adds.

"Is the car okay?" Isabelle asks. "Did you hit something?"

"No. We rolled it very carefully down the bluffs and then we drove it home."

"Oh my God! We have to get you to a hospital."

"No, Isabelle. I'm too weak and my arms are all fuzzy." Harry clutches his chest and throws himself on the sofa. "Don't stop. You guys look sexy kickboxing each other."

"You were fighting," Martine says sternly. "Harry, Guy has a broken leg and he's much older than you. He's never been very strong."

"Martine, please do me a favor and don't defend me," Guy says. "We weren't fighting each other. We rolled the car down the bluffs just like Harry said." Guy collapses onto the other end of the couch by Harry's feet.

Martine crosses her arms over her chest. "Are you both okay?"

"Yes," says Harry.

"Did you at least get all the stuff?"

"Yes. Did you tear up the money?"

"Yes, we did. And we cleaned the stretchers. And I made sandwiches for lunch. So let's eat in here and watch the rest of my show and then we'll start."

STE-FAMILLE

Down on the south bank of the Chenal de l'Île d'Orléans, cobalt morning glories unfurl on the walls of l'Hôtel d'Argenson. A brass plaque beside the wide doorway explains that, like the other stone houses in Ste-Famille, this building was erected by the French regime in the seventeenth century. With no one there to read it, the modern-looking plaque lends the wide doorway of the hotel an atmosphere of the uncanny.

The maids are in the kitchen, ironing tablecloths and boiling water. The cook collects balls of dough that have risen on the counter under checkered cheesecloths, and slides the dough on wood paddles into the brilliant maw of the oven. A smell of frying potatoes unwinds in the warming air. The whine of the radio anchorman's voice is caught halfway between stations, interpreting the weather, interrupting the silence.

Upstairs, the paneled hallways and wallpapered bedrooms are largely silent, except for a persistent knocking on the heavy oak door of room 12, behind which sleep Jules and Jim.

Jim leans up to turn on the lamp. He slides into his slippers and robe and ties the striped silk belt around his waist. As he treads toward the door he glances out the window at the expanse of strawberry fields. The knocking continues. He feels annoyed that there is no peephole in the door.

"Qu'est-ce que vous voulez?" he calls.

"Ouvrez la porte, monsieur. It's the police."

He swallows. "Is there a problem?"

"Ouvrez la porte. Je suis—Nous sont les police."

"Please, speak English if you can't speak French," he says as he opens the door.

"Police officers are required in this district to be bilingual, not to be francophones."

Jim studies the two young men in uniform. One has bad skin masked by a thick layer of flesh-colored Clearasil. He wears dark glasses and a hat with the visor pulled down low. The slighter of the two is less absurd, although he has a brown leather belt hitching up oversized pants.

"What would you like?" Jim inquires.

"Would you mind letting us in? You can shut the door. I'm Constable Vurko and this is Constable Kirkland."

Jim steps back from the door, smiling.

"Ask your friend to get out of bed."

Jules stands out of the sheets, allowing the men a brief glimpse of his tall, naked length before he draws a red velvet robe with red satin stripes over his broad shoulders. The slim man nods to the strange man, who begins opening and searching drawers in the antique bureau. Jim watches his face, reflected in the speckled mirror over the bureau. He feels that this one is familiar to him in spite of the disguise. Jim frowns at the quick and careless way this one fumbles through the drawers.

"What are you looking for?" Jim asks. "We can make it quicker for you if you tell us."

"Have you been to the United States recently, or has your companion been to the United States recently, Monsieur Mann?" the slim one inquires, flipping open a small notebook and posing with his pen on the page.

"We travel back and forth between Québec and the U.S. on business all the time."

"What sort of business do you do?"

"Tell your friend to tell me what he is looking for," Jim says sharply.

"Only one underwear drawer."

"I would like to see a warrant."

"We have a warrant for the entire hotel. We have information that a large-scale purchase of counterfeit American dollars has taken place in this hotel and that you and Mr. Legrand have those bills in your possession."

"Monsieur Legrand and I deal in furniture. We are resting a few days before going back to work. We like to fish, and there are lovely trout routes along the St. Lawrence. Please, don't touch my shaving kit. That was a gift." These boys, these stupid boys, he thinks.

The slim one looks over at Jules, who stands, solid in his slippers, with his arms folded over a wide chest. His eyes are slightly hooded, but amber-colored irises glimmer through translucent eyelashes. His wrinkled neck supports a firm jaw that has lost little definition over time. He has very large, round cheekbones and a high forehead. Only the thinness of his darkly veined calves, beneath the loosely fastened robe, betrays some weakness to his body.

"Maybe you weren't involved," the slim one starts again, nervous. "If you told us that, and you showed us where you found the money, I'm sure the Crown attorney would let you continue with your . . . *honeymoon.*"

"Psychology is an art," Jim says slowly, "practiced with fanatic regularity by amateurs. There is no money here. Perhaps you have the wrong room."

"Perhaps we do. Constable, take Mr. Legrand into the bathroom while I have a talk with Mr. Mann."

The disguised man steps toward Jules, who waits for a nod from Jim before he treads to the ensuite.

In the bathroom, Axel leans against the closed door. Jules stands with his back to the ivory-colored Jacuzzi, returning the young man's gaze. After a minute he says, "You're obviously not the police. Who are you?"

Axel smiles. Jules notices that his two front teeth are broken, making his grin look like a baring of fangs.

"Are you deaf? I asked who you are. What do you want?"

"We're going to help you retire."

Jules smiles. "You think you're going to kill me? And then what? Do you think that you can go to work in my place? Do you know who we work for?"

"You could work for my mother, for all I care. We're not here to take your place. We're here to take what you have."

"You're the freelancers. Let me tell you a secret, boy. All young men think they can strike out on their own. But sooner or later you need someone to insure your actions. You need to know that you can fuck up and come back to work tomorrow—or that you will get something extra when you prove yourself. It's okay. We all need someone to tell us where to go and what to do and why. It's too much work, it's too much strain, to try and do it all yourself."

"That's what you think."

"Very eloquent. Why not let us buy you off, then?"

"Because we want it all."

Jules nods and then, just as he hears a crash and a high yelp from the other room, he lowers his head and braces his neck by raising his shoulders. In one move he leaps across the bathroom and jams his skull beneath the young man's chin, slamming his head against the door. He grabs the young man's arm, twists it around and stretches it out and punches him in the back of his elbow. The young man cries out, grabs the baton strapped to his belt and hits at Jules as he falls to the ground. He flails, striking wildly as Jules knocks his arms away. He tries to hit Jules in the shoulder, the face. Jules grabs Axel by the head and wrenches his neck. Axel lashes back and hits Jules in the side of the neck. Jules steps back and his foot lands on a damp towel. He slips and crashes to the floor. He strikes his temple on the side of the tub. His temple crumples and his brown eyes roll back as shards of bone spear his brain. Then he lies there, a dead bull in the bathroom. His striped silk robe falls open to reveal a muscled body covered with gray hair.

Axel staggers to his feet, clutching his twisted arm. He swings the door open and calls to his partner. Rob looks over from the bedroom. He is having trouble standing. He has a broken lip and his chin is red. Jim looks past Axel, and something in his posture collapses. He staggers to the doorway of the bathroom and looks at Jules motionless on the clean tiles. He sees the way the neck is bent, the face balancing the weight of the great skull on the floor. The gold band on the finger looks tight beneath the swollen knuckle.

"Please," Jim murmurs. "Kill me too." He turns to face a gun.

"You see that? You see my neck? That old fudge-packer hit me hard. Did you look at his shoulders? He must've looked like a boxer back before the juice ran out of his sausage."

"Shut up, Axel. There's nothing here. There's no real money to buy the fake money and there's no fake money to sell. I don't believe it! We hit them too early. Shit!"

"Did you look around to see if they wrote down a place or a time anywhere?"

The two men begin tearing apart drawers and cupboards for a notebook, a diary, anything that might contain the plan of action that they failed to retrieve from the two men lying on the bathroom floor. Rob holds up something that he pulled from the breast pocket of a suit jacket.

"Axel, look. Here's a Visor organizer. It has a password lock. Did one of them have any kids or pets? Do you see any pictures around?"

Axel snaps his fingers repeatedly, trying to produce a memory as a magic trick. "Mann has a daughter. He was married a long time ago. What do you call it? Wearing a beard. What's her name? What's her name? Ashley. Addy? No, Ainsley. No, Frenchie name, *Chloe*, small tits, short legs, juicy ass. I saw them together once, in a restaurant on St. Catherine Street. Yeah, that girl has an ass like a song."

"That's it, Chloe. A legendary hit man like Jim Mann and he still types his daughter's name in every time he checks his calendar. You know what my password is?"

"What?"

"Modigliani."

"What is that, a pasta?"

"I have *no* idea. That's what makes it a great password."

The boat sits low in the water. Jules and Jim are wrapped in burlap, stretched out between the seats. Axel and Rob face each other on the narrow benches over the bodies. Axel rows. The sunlight catches a set of ripples, sending a pattern of light across the lake surface. Bands of clouds gather overhead. Axel pulls in the oars and drops them on the bodies, stretching and massaging his forearms.

"It's funny," he says quietly, squinting at the sky.

"What's funny?"

"Killing these two old guys. It's like killing my own dad again."

"Say again?"

"I said *killing* these old guys reminds me of my dad, of killing my dad, like if I were to do it all again."

"Why? Would you do it differently?" Rob says. He removes a foil package from his shirt pocket and pushes a cigarette through tight lips.

"No." Axel sniffs at the tobacco smoke.

"Was he a prick?"

"No. Well, maybe sometimes. Stubborn, you know how they get. He just got on my nerves. He moved in with me in this little flat in Beaconsfield where there was barely room for me and the rats. He was on his own because my mother left him. For no reason, he said. But he was always yelling. One day I told him to keep his fuckin' voice down or I was gonna punch him in the mouth. But he just kept yelling so I told him one more time, you shut up, you big-mouthed gorilla, shut up or I'm going to punch you in your big mouth. But he just wouldn't stop. So I shot him in the face, finished my Wheaties and went back to bed. Had the best sleep of my life."

"Why'd you kill him? You said you were going to punch him."

"Yeah, but I'd have to punch him all the time." He glances down at the large shapes beneath the burlap. He gives one of them a light kick. "These two old guys, you know, they were the biggest baddies in Québec when I was a kid. When they were collectors for the Guillaimés they used to carry bats with nails hammered through them. They used to smack people in the face with those spiked bats if they didn't pay on time. Blinded at least a few guys. Killed a woman once for screaming at them while they worked on her husband; she was begging them to stop. Jules Legrand and Jim Mann, look at 'em, killers."

They let the boat rock and ignore each other for a few minutes. Out of nowhere Axel suddenly recalls his father's cocoa. The only time that noisy fart was silent was when he was making cocoa on the gas stove.

He remembers sitting on a stool, watching those big hands break bars of chocolate into pieces. Sometimes his dad bought blocks of chocolate from the candy factory. That's right, he didn't yell when he was driving either. He wore a brown hat and Axel sat beside him in the car. They drove to the candy factory. Axel waited in the car, staring at the brick walls, tilting his head to the left and to the right. And soon his father came out with a clear plastic bag holding a block of chocolate as dark as his leather coat. At home, Axel climbed on a stool while his dad chipped the chocolate with a knife and a hammer. And then slowly, slowly, slowly the chocolate melted and the milk was added, skimmed and stirred. Into two apple-green mugs with a crackled glaze his father poured the cocoa. Whatever chips were left on the counter, his dad drew off with the side of his hand, pulling the sweet whiskers into his palm and dusting his palms over the mugs so that flecks and lines of pure chocolate melted on the shimmering surface of the cocoa.

A sudden image of his father's expression of surprise and the crimson trickle of blood passing over his nose propels him back to the present.

"So, what are we going to do? How are we gonna get the money now?"

"His Visor said that they had plane tickets booked to New Jersey for Saturday. After we dump the bodies we'll hang out in their room and wait for the counterfeiters. I guess we can just leave their bodies in the room. Everyone will think that these old guys decided to split a bikini and retire to Cuba. Get out the fishing gear. There's another boat over there."

He flips the burlap back and looks at Jules. His hooded eyes are open but they look flat and dry. Pulling two fishing rods out from under Jules, Axel must push the body with one foot to extricate the lines. A hook catches in Jules's hand.

Beneath the water's surface, silence dislodges time. Minutes gather without meaning. A school of tiny fish skims two silent faces. There they are, all that's left of Jules Legrand and Jim Mann, killers.

The muffler of a bronze Chrysler clatters, dragging on the cobblestones. Vieux Montréal, 1967. Drunken teenagers stumble down the narrow alleys past overflowing carts of flowers. They wave red-and-white banners and release orange balloons that flow up into the sky. The crowd parts when a car horn bleats. The windshield is spattered with bright, fresh blood. Jules and Jim, young again, laugh behind cracked glass. Jules turns on the windshield wipers and water dilutes the blood, which runs, soapy and pink, before being streaked across the glass by the wiper blades.

Red lights spiral on the roof of a tow truck in the parking lot outside a motel. A ceiling fan revolves over an unmade bed.

Jim perches on the edge of the bed, counting out dollars. Jules half lies, half leans on the covers, breathing clouds of smoke from an American cigarette into a tumbler of Canadian whiskey.

"Talk to me. Keep me awake," he mutters. He wipes sweat from his forehead with his forearm. "*Criss*, I cut my hand, throwing that woman onto the car. Hostie! Was she carrying a knife?"

"Mon Dieu, c'est profond, ma souris. Assieds-toi sur le lit. Je prendrai soin de lui."

Jim rises and walks to the bathroom. He twists the chrome taps and runs water over a hand towel. Jules collapses onto his back on the bed with his legs over the side.

"Séverine will be happy. You'll bring home a bag of bread today."

"Ne parle pas de Séverine. Donne-moi ta main."

Jules raises his hand and closes his eyes. Jim wipes the blood away. He bends his head to kiss the wound.

In the rocking chair beside the open bedroom window, Séverine sleeps with Chloe. The bright sun shines through the chair's open back, highlighting the limits of Séverine's body. Jim closes the door as softly as possible and sits on the floor to take off his shoes.

"Séverine, réveille-toi."

"Why? I'm sleeping."

"Oui, ma chère. Le bébé aussi."

"Speak English, Jim. I want her to speak good English."

"Mais ses parents sont français."

"But the world speaks English, Jim. I want her to speak like a lady lawyer, not like a poor Catholic girl, begging her boss at the market for a raise. It's a country speaking two languages."

"If you want her to speak beautifully you don't teach her English. And this is not a bilingual country. *Langue sacrée des pauvres*," he coos at Chloe. "Nous avons une langue pour l'amour, une langue pour la famille, et une langue pour l'argent."

His wife muffles a laugh with her hand. "You have a bad day, Jim? Everything go all right?"

"Everything is good. I'm taking her to her room."

In the hallway Chloe flexes her shoulder muscles and her chin trembles. Her brow crumples as she softly frets.

"Shh. Shh, Chloe. You're so hot. You're a little oven. Ne pleure pas, chaton. Tu, tu es vraiment au centre de mon coeur."

"English, Jim," Séverine calls out. "J'écoute."

"Don't tell your mother, Chloe," he whispers. "Don't tell anyone. Mon petit chaton triste, tu es vraiment au centre de mon coeur. Tu es seule. Chloe, let me look at your little fingers. Oh, Chloe, you are beyond me. Even when my heart stops, I will still remember you."

RAVEL

"Come out."

Martine leans on the bathroom door. Guy is inside, washing up and shaving. He watches his reflection in the mirror, assesses his resistance with pride.

"I'm almost done. I'll be out in a minute," he says finally.

"Well, come down to the basement when you're ready."

"Ready for what?"

"When you're ready to start working," she calls out and starts to walk away.

Guy opens the bathroom door. His face is half-masked by shaving cream. "Let's talk," he says.

Naked to the waist, he leans into his own image in the mirror and ignores her for a few minutes. He shakes off the razor blade in the dirty sink water. He wipes his face with a towel, which he throws on the floor. Martine arches her eyebrows.

"I want you to leave Isabelle behind," Guy says, turning to her. "I want you to leave her here with Harry and I'll take you to Ste-Famille. This will be the last time, okay? This will be the last crime. I'll go back to Boston and pack my things and drive them here and get a job. I'll take care of you. Isabelle can go to school, to university. She's a smart girl. Harry can go on with his life. I'll help you do this once and then it's over. I'm going to negotiate with you and make us a life like the life we should have had from the beginning."

She tilts her head, looking at his cast and then at the floor.

"Martine? Are you listening to me?"

She smiles. "Your tale, sir," she says slowly, "would cure deafness. How long have you been practicing to tell me about this takeover?"

"That's not what I want."

"You're in my house, Guy. You can't change the way I run my life. You know, this is not a game we play. We don't do this because we're lazy. You think I dragged Isabelle into a life of crime. But I didn't corrupt my daughter. I believe I did the right thing. Sally and I were with her day and night. She was involved in everything we did. She was never alone, she was never lonely. You know, even people who have had violent childhoods, as we did, Guy, know that childhood, at least here in North America, is supposed to be free of work, free of worry. Childhood is when you feel loved for nothing, for existing. Why give them that . . . that experience if every day of the rest of their lives will be so different? Do you think working as a bank teller, blowing the bank manager for a raise, is going to solve all her problems? I want her here, with me, happy. I want to be happy too."

"You've never been happy."

"That doesn't matter. It's still what I want. See, I also want things that I can't have."

"Martine, try to see my point of view. Please, just let me have some effect by being here. Let me do something to help you. Let me matter."

"No, Guy. The answer is still no."

The white arc of a contrail dissolves across the sky. Harry swallows the blade of grass between his teeth and rolls on his side to face Isabelle.

"Izzy. Izzy, wake up, sleepy head. It's time to take the paper back inside."

Isabelle stretches her arms over her head and yawns, arching her back. She and Harry are lying on an inflatable mattress in the backyard. The weighed-down sheets are all around them, like the square waves of a paper ocean. They have slept outside all night. Isabelle notices that her clothes and skin feel damp. She rolls to face Harry and says, "Did you sleep all right?"

"Yes, after the mosquitoes disappeared."

"They don't bite me."

"They must. You look so tasty. You must be one of the rare people who aren't allergic to the bites."

"Then why don't I feel them biting me?"

"Because their saliva contains something to dull the pain. Since you don't get itchy, they can drink your blood all night."

She grimaces and sits up. Squinting at the sun, she calculates that it must be close to ten o'clock. "Why did you let me sleep so long?"

"The paper still wasn't dry yet. You were snoring. And when I put sunscreen on you, you didn't even open your eyes."

"Thanks. Let's look at it."

Isabelle shifts off of the mattress and stands.

"Don't look, Izzy."

"Why?" Isabelle looks around. She feels her heart swing like a pendulum in her chest. She gasps. The sheets are too thick; they have rippled in the sun. But worse, they are speckled with bird shit and grass seeds.

"Oh fuck," she hisses.

"I haven't been able to get up the nerve to go inside and tell Martine."

"Oh shit," Isabelle exclaims. She hugs her rib cage tightly and then presses a tight fist to her lips. "Shit!" she yells.

Broken glass litters the floor in the center of the room. Martine, Guy, Isabelle and Harry circle the broken vase. Wildflowers lie in a puddle.

"Mom?"

"Don't say anything. Just let me think."

"We could go buy more lumber and make more screens."

"There isn't enough pulp."

"We could shred our books and clothes."

"We can't cook it fast enough."

"Martine," Guy starts, "we could make as much money as possible from the remaining pulp and fill the bottom of the bag with newspapers."

"They count the money, Guy. If they have to bring back a light buy, they'll bring back bodies with it."

"Mom."

"Shut up, Isabelle."

"Can't we use the ruined stuff to make the paper again?" Guy asks.

"We can't get the bird shit out," Harry tells him. "The mixture will be too lumpy and it won't go through the printer. I should have put a plastic sheet over them. I was afraid it wouldn't get completely dry."

Martine moves, agitated, toward the counter. As she walks she steps on a piece of glass. She swears and falls to the floor. No one speaks. She lifts her foot to extract the broken glass. Blood paints her fingers; she shakes her hand and blood flies from her fingertips.

"I should have cut my throat when you walked through the door," she shrieks at Guy.

Harry swallows loudly. "Don't be so cruel, Martine. We haven't got time to hurt each other."

———————

Two tellers are on duty at the bank. Martine joins the single line filing between the ribbons toward the front. The vents hiss from the pressure of air-conditioning set high. There are four people ahead of her. An old man holds his checkbook between quivering hands that poke out from the overlong sleeves of a faded jacket. A young Asian woman rocks from foot to foot with a baby asleep over her shoulder. A tall man stares at the ceiling, hands in his pockets, dark hair showing gray. Martine follows his gaze to a yellow water stain. She watches a rusty drop of water quiver and fall to the floor. The teenage girl directly ahead of her wraps her goose-bumped arms around her body. Her white shirt is almost transparent under the fluorescent lights. A black bra segments her narrow back.

The line moves quickly. Martine watches the teenage girl walk up to the counter and place a slip of a paper in front of the female teller. The teller examines the paper and then walks into an open vault.

"Next," the other teller calls.

Martine looks over at him. He nods at her and then frowns. "Next," he says again. She looks into the vault and sees the woman teller unwrapping a package. "Ma'am?"

"I want to wait for her," Martine says.

He stares vacantly, sighing. No one has come in after Martine.

A minute passes. The teenage girl leaves. Martine is alone with the man and woman behind the counter. She moves haltingly toward the woman teller.

"Can I help you?" the girl prompts.

Martine's legs weaken beneath her. The cold sweat on her back and chest makes her shiver. "I'm here to—" she starts and then coughs. "I'm sorry. I'm here. I'm trying to—"

"Yes?" the girl prompts. She has blond hair tied back in an elaborate bun. Peachy streaks of blush on her cheeks make Martine feel queasy.

"Do you have an account here?"

"No."

"Did you want to open an account?"

"No."

"What do you want?"

"Money," Martine whispers.

"Just a minute." Her heels click as she steps back. She walks to an office sequestered behind the counter and off to the side of the vault. Martine stares into the vault but all she sees is gleaming steel.

The worried-looking girl returns with an older woman in a black suit. "This is our manager," she says.

"Is there a problem?" the manager asks politely.

Martine looks at the older woman's face. Cataracts give her eyes a feline glint, one shimmering pupil bleeds slightly into the pale iris. Her features suddenly gather into a familiar visage. "Claire," she says. "Claire Chabrol," as if the name contained a great deal of information.

"Come into my office, Martine. You look sick. Sit down for a minute."

She pushes a section of the counter open, and Martine follows Claire into a tiny office. Claire shuts the door and steers her into a chair.

"What are you doing here?" Claire asks. "I've never seen you here before. Are you all right?"

Martine clears her throat and looks at Claire through a wash of tears. "I came to rob the bank," she says. "I'm here to rob you." Her voice breaks. "We couldn't make enough money. I need eighty thousand American dollars. I have a gun in my purse."

"You don't have a purse."

"I have a gun in—" She looks at her knees. Her legs are shaking so badly her knees are bumping up and down.

Claire puts two hands on Martine's shoulders. "Steady," she says.

"We don't have enough money," she sobs. "The paper is ruined. They'll kill us if we don't bring all the money to Ste-Famille. I don't see what else I can do, Claire. You have to let me rob you. You have insurance. I know that if I had a gun you would have to give me the money with no argument, for your own safety and—" She gasps for breath.

"I can't, Martine. I'm the bank manager now and it's a federal crime to rob a bank."

"Oh for fuck's sake, so is counterfeiting."

"Shh, quiet. Let's keep it down while we talk. The tellers will call the security guard in from the parking lot if they hear you. He's only walking around the building."

"I have to rob you. You have to say that I robbed you. Please, Claire. Please, I'm begging you. Get me the money and let me out and then call the police and stall them for me. I'll take Izzy and we'll go to Ste-Famille, pay off our contacts and stop. We'll run away and we'll stop all of this. I'll get a job."

"I can give you a job. You can work here. Can't you arrange something?"

"No, it's too late. They won't believe me. They'll think that I'm keeping it or I sold part of it to someone else. Their own bosses will blame them for the missing money. Even if I try to explain, they'll still kill us."

"Okay. Okay, calm down. I'm going to help you. Sally helped me and you know I'm going to help you. Take a breath, you're hyperventilating. Breathe slowly. Hold your breath. Now let it out. Can I call the police for you?"

Martine shakes her head. She gags and gasps and puts her head between her knees. Her arms fall helplessly to her sides. "You're not listening to me. I'm here to rob you. I'm robbing you."

Claire kneels in front of Martine and strokes her hair. "No, you're not."

"Yes, *I am*."

"No, you're not that kind of criminal. I want you to pull yourself together and walk out of the bank. Go and sit in the coffee shop across the street and wait for me. Do just as I tell you. Go wait for me. I'll take my break and meet you there."

Martine lifts her head and moans, "I should have brought a gun."

The coffee shop is crowded with elderly people drinking tea. Walkers fill the spaces between tables. Martine takes the only empty deuce. She leans her head sideways against the wall and starts to cry. She waves the waitress away, shaking her head and covering her eyes. The waitress comes back a minute later with a cup of coffee and a plain doughnut on a chipped plate.

"It's free," she says gently. All the wizened faces in the room heliotrope like sunflowers toward Martine.

The coffee cools. Martine sips and coughs; the cream is slightly curdled. Behind the counter the waitress polishes bent cutlery. A bell signals, and Claire slips into the seat across from her.

"You forgot your purse," Claire says loudly. She places a large red leather handbag on the table and pushes it toward Martine, who stares.

"What have you done?" Martine says softly. "What did I make you do?"

As she releases the mug of coffee it tips and spills. Rushing over, maternally clucking, the waitress pulls napkins from a steel container and begins sopping up the brown liquid. She dabs at Martine's legs where the coffee runs over the edge of the table and onto her skirt. "Are you all right?" she asks. "You aren't burned?"

"I'm good." She pushes the waitress's hands from her lap. "I'm good. It's all right. I'm sorry about the coffee."

"I can bring you another."

"No. I have everything I need."

"Can I bring you anything?" the waitress asks Claire.

"Bring us two glasses of Coke with lots of ice," she answers as she nudges something against Martine's leg beneath the table. Martine reaches a hand down and her fingers close around a tiny bottle.

"You need to pull yourself together. Have a drink with me and I'll explain what you should do."

Martine feels her head nodding, her mind spinning inside it. As she looks at Claire Chabrol sitting across from her in a neat white blouse and a navy jacket and skirt, she sees the same woman but younger, stripped of the diamond rings on her fingers and the gold hoops in her pierced ears, propped up in the tub, loose limbs submerged in soapy water, and Sally, at her most together, leaning in and tending with alcohol and gauze, gently dressing a livid cut across the woman's face. But this woman, she's so different. She sits straight and calm behind what seems like a giant red leather bag. Deep grooves on either side of her nose travel down to her mouth. Her hair is short and white, tucked behind her ears. Her blue eyes gaze steadily back.

"There is eighty thousand dollars in American one-hundred-dollar bills in that bag," Claire says. She falls silent as the waitress approaches and deposits two glasses of Coke on the table. When the waitress turns away both women crack the little metal caps from their liquor bottles and discreetly pour rum into the Coke. Martine sips through a straw. The rum singes her sinuses.

"It's all right for a few days, maybe weeks," Claire continues. "I took it from a safety deposit box owned by an older gentleman. He never checks on it. I think it's supposed to go to his children after his death. If you to take it to Ste-Famille and sell it as counterfeit with the other counterfeit money and bring me back all the money you get from selling it, I can replace it. If you can't bring back enough I'll cover the difference and you can work it off. I'll find some way to convert it all back to U.S. currency without it being traced, I don't know how yet. Then the money goes back in the box and I'll give you a job at the bank, and we'll put all of this behind us. Okay? We'll get you a fresh start, forget everything that's happened at your house the last forty years, and just start again. Your mother did what she had to do to take care of you. Sally used the only resources she had, but you have other choices. Sally took care of everyone the best she could, and she saved my life. I don't want you to ever forget that your mother saved my life."

"Thank you," Martine breathes.

"Cheers."

Chickadees rise from the trees. The car weaves along the road. As the horizon swallows the last radiant sliver of the sun, the atmosphere is gilded pink. Martine pulls the car into the driveway, turns the ignition off and grabs the leather bag.

Harry, Isabelle and Guy are sitting in a row on the sofa in the living room. Harry stands as she enters.

"I've got it," she says. "I've got the rest of the money."

"Where?"

She drops the bag on the coffee table in front of them. Isabelle leans forward and unbuckles the bag. She pulls out a fistful of hundred-dollar bills. "Are they real or counterfeit?" she asks.

"They're counterfeit," Martine says. "I had it hidden in Estérel."

Isabelle's gaze snaps to her mother's face but she stays quiet.

"I'm going to have a drink. Does anyone want one?" Martine heads for the kitchen without waiting for an answer.

Guy can't stop staring at the paper bills in the open bag. Pressure builds in his forehead, between his eyebrows. Frowning so hard makes his eyes ache. Isabelle follows her mother into the other room. Harry stands at the window, trying to look out at the backyard, facing his own reflection. The ticking clock echoes Guy's beating heart. He stands quietly, lifts the bag and walks to the staircase. At the staircase he pauses and waits for someone to call him back. He hears nothing, so he steps on the first stair. His cast bumps the back of the next step. He makes his way loudly up the stairs. One quiet soft foot, one loud hard cast. At the top of the stairs he pauses and looks down the hall at the open bathroom door.

Inside the bathroom Guy moves quickly, locking the door as he hears Martine begin to call and the three together running up the stairs. Madly, he shreds the bills, dropping the pieces into the toilet bowl. He flushes, and the whirling mass of water carries away the mutilated presidents. Shaking water from his arm, he grabs another handful, shredding while he waits for the vortex to calm, and then he flushes another batch of money down. Martine, Isabelle and Harry pound on the door, calling to him, "Guy, Guy, what are you doing? Stop! Oh my God, Guy, stop. You don't know what you're doing."

He flushes again. A body slams against the door. The knob shakes beneath a hand. He flushes another handful down the toilet.

"Guy!" Martine screams. "It's real money! It's real. My mother's friend stole it for me and I have to give it back. Guy, please!"

Suddenly the presidents' faces stare back at him reproachful as they are sucked down the drain. He grabs the plunger from beside the toilet and begins pumping just as the bathroom door breaks off its hinges and crashes to the floor. Harry drags him bodily into the hall. Isabelle and Martine fish with bare hands at the few pieces that have floated up with the regurgitated water. Martine slumps beside the toilet and stares at him, where he lies outside the door.

"What have you done?" she says. "Why did you do it?"

An hour passes and the room grows dark. They are all still sitting or lying on the floor, not speaking. Finally, Martine closes the lid of the toilet and says, "I'm going down to the lake."

Isabelle grabs her hand.

"It's all right, Isabelle, I'm not going to hurt myself. I just want to be alone to think for a while."

Martine steps over Guy in the hall. He sits up to watch her as she walks downstairs. When he turns back to the bathroom, Isabelle is staring at him with huge, red eyes.

"You've killed us!" she sobs.

Martine clicks her flashlight off to watch the moon rise. She searches the capacious pockets of her skirt for cigarettes and a match. The sound of the match lighting strikes into the crickets' song. She watches the tear-shaped flame subside, flicks the match away and lights another. Inhaling the smoke makes her head throb. Her lungs feel strained. She holds her breath and then lets it out slowly, watching the smoke coil and dissipate. The moon is nearly half full, an almost perfect semicircle spooned by its shadow in the sky. Stars glow timidly in the gathering dusk. Martine rubs the palm of her free hand over the engraving of her mother's name, feeling the warmth leave her hand. Water rushes over the shore like a sheet thrown across a bed. Somewhere, a boat must have passed.

As she throws the butt of her cigarette into the lake she hears a soft crepitation in the bushes.

"Guy?"

"How did you know it was me?"

Pale moths dangle in the flashlight beam. Guy picks his way over smaller stones until he reaches the base of the boulder. Martine moves over to make room.

"It's no use," he complains when he is seated beside her. "My cast is wet."

She responds with lengthy silence.

"I'm sorry, Martine."

"It's all right. It's not really your fault. I told you the money was counterfeit. Do you want a cigarette?"

"Sure. Don't laugh at me if I cough."

"Here. Are Isabelle and Harry all right?"

"I don't know. What do you mean by all right?"

"Hm, well, here we are. How much money did you flush down the toilet?"

"A lot. Maybe ten thousand. There's still at least seventy thousand in the bag. I have ten thousand in my bank account.

I can have it wired to me and we can top up the money and still sell it."

"No. That was a bad idea." She taps her lower lip with the filter of her cigarette. "I tried to rob the bank."

He shivers but holds back the flow of questions.

"I tried to rob the bank." She shrugs. "But it was too upsetting. So, it turns out Claire Chabrol, this woman that Sally helped years ago, is now the manager at the bank I tried to rob. I guess she felt like she had to help me. So she stole this money and told me to pay her back after we sold it as counterfeit. She was going to give me a job at the bank when we finished the deal. It sounds crazy now. A couple of hours ago it sounded really good."

"We have to give her the money back."

"I know. I can't drag anyone else into this."

She takes out another cigarette, lighting it in her cupped palm to protect it from the breeze. "Well, so much for good intentions," she says, shaking the match.

"I told you I can get the rest of the money. I'll write her a check and we'll take the bag back to her tonight. She can add my money to the rest of the money. I had a small inheritance from my mother. It won't leave me much, but I don't care. We'll figure out what to do about the rest of it. We'll figure it out together."

"Okay. But I don't want you to come with me to Claire's. I want you to pack your things and get ready to leave the house. I'll take the money back to Claire. And then I'll get you Isabelle's passport. And you take her with you to Boston.

Harry and I will go to Ste-Famille alone. I need to meet with them by myself. We've been dealing with the same two men for years. They're old guys. They used to be killers, but who knows." She gives a miserable short laugh.

"I want to be the one who goes with you, Martine. Let Harry take Isabelle to Boston. I'll give them the address and the keys to my mother's apartment and we'll meet them there. I can't let you go without me."

"I've been going without you for years."

"I know, that's why I want to be the one to go with you now."

"They've never seen you before. It's always been Sally and me. If you come instead it will look bad from the moment we walk in the door. That's funny, I've never planned so much for the future before. For me, time usually begins in the present and extends maybe two identical weeks into the future before it just disappears again."

Guy clears his throat. "That must have made it easier to deal with what you do."

She glances at him. "You mean the counterfeiting. Yes, I guess it makes some things easier. But I was never really bothered by it. I guess no one ever really sees themselves as a criminal. You know me, I thought I had a system of thought that made sense of it all. If you buy goods manufactured in another country by starving children, that's theft, but it's not illegal. If you take another person's job when they become too old or too sick to work, that's a kind of manslaughter. My whole idea was to stay away from those kinds of crimes, to stay out of the crimes that make me sick by inventing my own economy. When I was standing in the bank line, I looked at the people in front of me and I realized that I had no idea what they were doing there. I couldn't even guess what their motives might be. Why put your money, if it is the most important thing to you, into the hands of strangers?"

"I suppose people are afraid of being robbed."

"Everyone gets robbed, Guy. That's the nature of money."

She glances at the open phone book on the passenger seat, double-checks the address, checks her face in the ruthless rearview mirror and grabs the leather bag from the backseat.

A bell chimes deep in the house. Martine leans her ear against the door and listens as she presses the doorbell again. Goose bumps itch along her bare arms. She turns and rests her head on the closed door, looking at the sky. One flexed limb of the Milky Way is clearly visible, adorned with unidentified jewels. Crickets sweetly saw the air. She hears muffled footsteps, and a voice on the other side of the door calls out, "Who's there?"

"It's me, Martine," she calls back.

"What do you want?"

"I want to give back the purse I borrowed from you. I don't need it."

The door falls open to a wide, dark hallway. Claire stands in a thin white dressing gown and bare feet. Her wiry hair is crushed against her head on the right side. Today, in her trim suit and makeup, she looked to be in her early sixties, but in the deep hours of the failing night she looks much closer to eighty.

"Come in."

Martine steps past her, brushing her body hip to hip. Claire shuts the door and walks down the hall without indicating if Martine should follow. Martine pads after her.

A long-haired calico cat lies on a frayed couch in the living room, flexing its claws in the fabric of an elaborate throw cushion. Martine takes a seat in the red velvet armchair beside the couch. The glass top of the coffee table is opaque with dust. Claire props her feet up on a stack of *Gazette*s on the floor beside the table. She does not turn on any lights. Martine's eyes gradually adjust.

"You have enough money now?" Claire asks in a hushed voice.

"Is someone else here?" Martine whispers back.

"Just Lola. The cat."

"Here's the bag," The chair makes a startling creak when Martine shifts. "I don't want to take your money in case we don't come back. I don't want you to end up in prison because you helped me."

Claire shrugs. "It's up to you."

"Well, here's the bag." She lifts it again. "There was an accident with some of the money and so I brought you a check to replace the amount I lost."

Claire studies the check, but she leaves the bag in Martine's hands. "You lost ten thousand dollars already? How did you do that?"

"It got flushed down the toilet. It was an accident."

"You're not very good with money," Claire says wryly. "So you're going to Ste-Famille without the money?"

"Yes. Unless Québec falls under martial law again, I think I still have to go."

"What do you think will happen to you?"

"I don't know." She puts the bag on the floor and reaches down to pet Lola's silky head. Lola trills and rubs her body aggressively against the two new bare legs in her living room.

"You look scared. I would be scared too. Let's think about this for a minute. You have a couple of options, you know. You can run away. Take Isabelle and whatever money you do have and walk away from that house, never go back. But they'll probably find you. I know enough about these people to know that they won't just walk away empty-handed. You can negotiate with them, tell them exactly what happened. Leave out the part about trying to rob the bank and losing ten thousand dollars down a toilet. That's what you're thinking of doing, isn't it? Do you know the names of all the people who are involved?"

"No. I only know the two men we deal with." Her throat is so tight she feels as if she's choking.

"That's bad. You should have kept control of that information. Your mother knew how to protect herself. Didn't she prepare you for something like this?"

"No. She might have thought we would stop after she was gone. She left us some money. But, as you said, I'm not very good with money."

"Okay, don't cry," Claire says softly. "I'm going to give you something and tell you what to do."

"No, Claire, I don't want you to be involved."

"It's too late. I'm already involved. As far as the police are concerned, I'm going to tell them that you came into the bank today and threatened my life. I got you the money you asked for and brought it to you across the street. I knew that you knew where I lived and I was afraid you would kill me. So I robbed the bank for you. Then you repented. You repented and at four a.m. you came to my house and you brought the money back. That way we both have an answer to why this bag went traveling today."

"Except for the ten thousand dollars."

"I have the check and I can cover up ten thousand dollars without taking a breath. Unlike you, I am good with money. Anyway, you repented, and I returned the money and reported what happened. The police will go to your house to arrest you but it will be burned to the ground."

"What?"

"Okay, you're right, that's too dramatic. They'll walk up to the door and knock. The dogs will be sniffing in the bushes."

"Dogs?"

"Okay, I'm just trying to have a little fun here. They'll knock, but you won't be there. You'll drive to Mexico with your daughter. And we'll never see you again. Or . . ."

"Or what?"

"Or you can take a gun with you to Ste-Famille. Shoot the bastards dead and walk away. Walk away from every minute that came before the minute when the last one falls. Get a fresh start."

"I can't kill anyone."

"You've never tried. I think you can. I believe in you, and I think it's the only way for you to save yourself and Isabelle. I think Sally would do it without talking it through, and I truly think that she would want you to kill these men and get out of this life. Anyway, forget what I think. Do you know how to use a gun?"

"No."

"Well, come into the yard with me. I'll give you my Ruger. It's small. It has an excellent silencer, the Quantum .22LR. The numbers are drilled so the gun can't be traced. My husband taught me a lot of useful things before he died. Come on, I'll get the gun and boil some water for tea. You look shattered. Then I'll teach you how to shoot. Martine, you have to be brave now. It's almost over. Take a lesson from your mother and me. You can do anything, anything at all, once you get rid of these men."

"They're just two old men."

"Two old men, well, that would be Jules and Jim. When I was twenty-one I met them once with Claude, in an underground bar in Old Montréal. Jim and my husband—that's Claude, you won't remember him—they had just met the week before. They were supposed to transport furs from Toronto to New York. They got as far as Buffalo and then Jim pulled the truck over behind a restaurant where the windows were barred. He told my husband to get out of the van and walk home. Claude was six-four, he weighed three hundred pounds, Jim was probably my height, five-seven, and I probably weighed more than he did. But Claude got out of the van. It was just a coincidence, us running into them at the bar.

I think Claude had been brooding since the night he hitch-hiked home from Buffalo. When I saw him looking at Jim I knew he was going to do something. He walked up behind Jim, grabbed his hair and slammed his forehead down on the bar. Jules stepped out of a crowd of men, all of them with identical sideburns and black turtlenecks. He grabbed Claude's hand. And I never saw the knife until he sliced the web of Claude's thumb to the bone. He twisted Claude's arm until he fell on his knees, and then Jules started sawing at the wrist. I threw myself at them. I threw myself on the floor, begging him to stop. Claude's blood was everywhere, on my arms and my dress, all over the floor, all over Jules. Claude passed out. I looked up and saw the other men lifting their beers and drinking.

"In the end I think Jules couldn't saw through the bones, the knife was too small, and so he lost his patience. My husband lay on the floor. I was beside him, screaming, cradling his hand in my lap. Jules looked at me and he actually smiled. These are not old men. These are old demons. They will kill you. No one will stop them. Don't even let them see you. You shoot them both in the back of their heads, drop the gun and run."

RAVEL

Streaks of sunlight bleach the sky. She picks a shoebox up from the passenger seat and leaves the car. The front door sticks and so she kicks it with her foot and then it opens. The stairs look dusty in the callow light. Martine steps out of her shoes and treads quietly down the hallway to the kitchen.

She lifts the kettle from the burner just as the whistle starts to hum. A chipped clay mug sits on the counter with a dry tea bag in the bottom. Martine pours the boiling water into the mug and sets the kettle back on the stove.

"What's in that box?"

Martine turns toward Isabelle's voice.

"You look awful, baby girl. Did you sleep at all?"

Isabelle stands in the doorway staring at the shoebox in the center of the table.

"No. What's in that box?"

"A pair of shoes."

Isabelle rubs her eyes with a fist and leans against the wall. Martine takes her mug from the counter and goes to the table, pulls out a chair for Isabelle and then sits in the chair beside it.

"Don't hold up the wall. Are Guy and Harry asleep?"

"Nobody has slept. Guy!" Isabelle calls over her shoulder.

"Wait, don't call them yet." Martine stirs the tea bag around in the water. "Sit," she says, gesturing to the chair.

Isabelle looks at the chair seat. She purses her lips and shifts her weight heavily from one foot to the other. "Why?" she says.

"Okay, I'll stand." Martine stands and they look at each other until Isabelle sighs and takes a seat in the kitchen chair. "Let me get you a pony of gin. You need to calm down and get some rest."

Isabelle props her chin in her hands and stares rigidly at the wall while her mother moves about behind her, gathering glasses and the gin bottle. She closes her eyes and listens to the freezer door opening and closing, the brittle cracking of the ice cubes being twisted from the tray, the tinkle of frozen water dropping into glass. Martine deposits two glasses and the bottle on the table. Isabelle keeps her eyes closed. She feels her mother's cool fingers in her hair, scratching her scalp gently and combing the silky strands. She can't help herself, she sniffles, and then coughs to disguise the sniffling. Tossing her head, she grabs the gin bottle and pours herself a drink.

"I love your beautiful hair," Martine says. Then, "That's the gin, not the tonic."

"I don't care," Isabelle mumbles, leaning the glass against her lips and draining it.

"It's very different without Sally here, isn't it?"

"What do you mean?" Isabelle says as she pours herself a more chaste portion of liquor. Martine takes the bottle to pour herself a dose.

"Things really fell apart this year. I wasn't able to keep everything organized the way Sally could."

A nerve twitches by Isabelle's mouth. She feels a line of pressure, like a little river of pain, flow narrowly from the edge of one tear duct to her temple. Her hands, clasped around the sweating tumbler, look anemic to her.

"It doesn't seem fair, does it? You didn't choose me to be your mother. Something that basic and you don't have any say." She sips her gin. "At least it can't be considered your failure, who your parents are."

"You didn't choose me either."

"I did. I made the choice. I chose to have you. I love you, Isabelle. I love you with everything. I love you and I'm responsible for you." Martine leans back in the creaky chair, contemplating the gin.

Ice in Isabelle's glass cracks; she feels the tiny shock against her palm. "I love you too."

"I know. I know you love me, baby girl. But you're not responsible for me. You're not responsible for anything I do. Okay, call the boys. We need to make a plan for what to do next."

"Guy, Harry!" Isabelle yells, suddenly impatient.

A few seconds later she hears footsteps on the stairs, in the hall and then the two men trail into the kitchen.

"My God, each of you looks worse than the last," Martine exclaims.

"Where did you go?" Harry asks.

"I went to see Claire. I gave her back the money and she helped me to come up with a plan. So this is the plan. Guy, I want you to drive me to Ste-Famille and then wait in the hotel room while I speak to Jules and Jim. Harry, I want you to stay here with Isabelle until we call you and then I want you to take a taxi to the train station and wait for Guy and me. Okay? It's very simple. We'll go to Boston. We're abandoning the house, but I don't want you to take anything that makes it look like you're moving. Does everyone understand? Everything will be all right, I'll make sure of it. But we need to hold it together and stay calm."

"What about the photographs?" Isabelle asks.

"Pick a few, maybe ten, and put them in your purse. Lots of people do that when they travel." She reaches forward and squeezes Isabelle's hand. She blinks when Isabelle pushes her hand away. "We'll be together," Martine says, "we'll take more pictures."

"I don't want to leave the pictures behind," Isabelle stares stubbornly at the wall. Tears roll down her flushed cheeks. "I won't leave them behind."

Martine clears her throat and shakes her head, annoyed. "They're only pictures."

"They're pictures of us, of Sally and us."

"Okay, bring an album, bring one album. You can always say that it's a gift for your grandmother in Boston. Fine, God, one album. Now I'm going to go upstairs and get some sleep. You all do the same. When we wake up all this will almost be over." Martine rises and exits, leaving behind a tumbler full of ice and a mug, steam winding up from viciously dark tea.

After a brief silence Guy follows her.

Harry and Isabelle look at each other.

"We're going to Ste-Famille, right?" she says.

Guy leans on the closed bedroom door and listens to Martine moving inside. He strokes the wood as if he could feel the outline of her body, trying to communicate his presence to her by touching the very outside of her room. He has done so many things wrong this evening. A cold marble of tension blocks his throat. He drags his fingers into a fist and hesitates before he knocks, barely grazing the wood with his knuckles.

Martine looks up toward the timid tapping. She looks around the room until she sees a wooden chest, lid open to reveal folded blankets and towels, at the foot of the bed. She walks to the chest and closes it quietly, slipping the brass lock through the brass loops and locking the blankets away. She pushes the chest along the floor until the door is blocked. As it hits the door the tapping ceases.

"Martine?" he says.

"Go to bed, Guy," she answers.

He presses his ear to the door but he can't hear anything beyond his own breathing.

Owls chant, drowsy in the quilted shadows of the trees. The sheets and blankets are bunched at the bottom of the bed, and Martine lies naked on her stomach at the very edge of the bed, one arm over the side and one hand stroking the cover of the closed shoebox. She stares at the shoebox, feeling her thoughts disintegrate. Before she sleeps she lifts the corner of the cardboard lid once more to stare at the silver weapon packed with odd socks in an old shoebox. As she drifts away, she imagines Claire's murmuring voice. "It's a Ruger pistol . . . Quantum .22LR suppressor . . . silencer . . . beautiful and re-liable . . . wipe the assembly . . . high-velocity ammunition . . . hammer the bastards . . . back of their heads . . . run, run . . . good gun . . . your mother . . . federal excise tax . . . suppressed rimfire bullets of sandblasted steel . . . yes, oh yes, such a good gun."

STE. FAMILLE

The waiter of La Fenouillère pauses politely at a distance from the table. He looks up at the mysterious atmosphere, at first just to look away from the couple, who are still caught in conversation together, and then to study the eerie yellow-gray light shining below roiling bands of clouds. Rippled peaks along the bands resemble rows of scales, and the shadows in between the bands resemble silver stripes. A mackerel sky, he thinks. He rocks in his stiff leather shoes, stroking the satin menu covers absently with his fingertips. He catches the odd word in spite of his determined distraction. "Tenebral." What does that mean? he wonders. Then "seashells . . . chocolate . . . all kinds of currants."

They're talking about food. They must be ready, he thinks, and he listens more closely.

"Money," the woman says, "is only a dream. Your life is only a dream. Even the dreamer of the dream is only a dream."

"How can you say that?" the man answers her. "How can there be a real dream without a real dreamer?"

"The dream," she explains, "it should be obvious, is only a dream. What do you want to drink?" Martine turns her head to the waiter, who shakes his head slightly, pretending that he has only just begun to listen.

"Monsieur?" the waiter leans toward Guy with a pen poised over a pad in his hand.

"Bring me a dark beer," Guy says.

"Let's share a bottle of wine," Martine suggests. "Let's have a nice bottle of wine and a special meal. What do you recommend?" she asks the waiter.

"Would Madame prefer white or red wine?"

"Red, something with teeth. Money is not an object." She winks at Guy. "I'd like a Barolo, if you have one."

He nods. "We do. And here are your menus."

"Don't give us the menus. Just give us the best food you have, all your favorite things."

"Everything is delicious here. Wait, I'll choose."

He places the notepad on the table and flips the menus into the air. For a second he stands, juggling the spinning satin rectangles; ribbons tied to the menus whirl. Then he throws them up in the air together and as they fall he claps his hands and catches them against each other. When he opens his palms the two folders open as one. He closes his eyes and puts a finger on the page, once, twice, three times.

"Canard au cassis, ravioli avec homard, pears and goat's cheese, and for dessert I will bring you a block of ice and hot maple taffy. You pour the taffy on the ice and peel it off, tastes divine." He puckers his lips as if to kiss someone.

A roll of thunder breaks the silence. Tiny raindrops spark across their skin. A green awning rolls slowly out over the patio. The motor purrs. The raindrops swell, splashing in the wine, until the awning cuts off their descent. The sound of drumming on the canvas harmonizes with the strumming of guitars drifting out from speakers hidden in the giant pots of palm trees. The lobster ravioli is creamy and mild, served in a single large bowl between Martine and Guy. She stabs a square of pasta and holds it out to feed him.

"Thanks," he says. "Why are we celebrating?"

She looks down at her side plate and pushes the sliced pear and endive into the chèvre with her fork. "We're not celebrating," she says quietly. "This is the calm before the storm. Don't think about it, Guy."

Thunder cracking in the sky reminds Guy of the sound of a baseball bat striking a metal post. Lightning causes a momentary shimmer of daylight. He sips his wine, feeling warm and relaxed, ready to trust the canvas awning.

"I like the calm before the storm," he says. "I think it's my favorite time. I could do without the storm." He leans forward. "Why don't we stay here tonight and drive to Mexico tomorrow? It could be perfect. I'll buy a ranch with the money my mother left me. We'll send for Isabelle and Harry and we'll raise chickens and horses. You'll wear long skirts that pick up the dust from the floor, and I'll walk funny, like a clown in giant pants."

She laughs and takes a sip of wine. "You're the second person to mention Mexico to me. You're tipsy. Eat your canard," she says.

"I'm not drunk; I'm just relaxed. I like the rain when I'm drinking wine. Okay, if we can't dream about escaping, then tell me what you remember about the day you chose me. Tell me about the first time we were together, from your point of view."

"Okay, let me think." She puts down her glass and wipes a red ring from the table with her finger. Lightning flickers again, softly, but there is a long pause before the muted thunder.

"It was summer," he prompts.

She nods. "It was summer. I hadn't seen you for a year or so. You were busy in high school and I was seducing men my own age at the bar in town, so we didn't cross paths much. I remember I had a dream a few months before the night I first took you. I woke up at three from that dream. I sat up in bed and I felt like . . . like I had suddenly identified a missing limb. Like I had known for some time that something about me was missing and suddenly I noticed it was my arms that were missing."

"What are you talking about? This is supposed to be the story of why you finally wanted me."

"It is. Let me finish. I sat up in bed and I knew I wanted to have a baby. I needed someone else in my life besides my mother to love me."

"I loved you."

"Not the same. I wanted someone to love me permanently. I wanted the kind of love that doesn't make you lonely. Anyway, you're missing the point. Do you want to hear the story or don't you?"

"Sorry."

"So I buried all my birth control pills in the garden. Then I took a shower and curled my hair. I braided the back and put on my mother's violet glass beads. I chose a dress, a white cotton apron-style dress. It was still too cool out to wear a dress like that, it was May. My breasts got hard in the wind as I rode my bicycle to Chantelle's. I had every intention of taking a lover that night, someone I knew a little bit, someone who had no family illnesses, someone who wouldn't love me. But once I was in the bar, leaning on the rail, sipping my beer and studying the candidates, I felt for the first time that it mattered who I slept with. It had never mattered before and, truth, it never mattered again. But those men, cheering and playing pool, that night they all seemed too fragile to me."

"But it was all right to choose me," Guy says, warming to humiliation, "even though I was sixteen. But not a grown man?"

"No, no, you weren't on my mind. I finished my drink and rode my bike home. The stars were brilliant as I rode underneath them. My headlight shone. It was this thin arm holding up my bicycle while I craned my head back to stare at the domed sky. I felt as if I had found myself inside a chandelier. It was a few months later that I went to visit your mother and found you at home. Pour me some more wine. Thank you."

Martine watches as Guy tilts the bottle, and the wine rolls in the bell, leaving translucent legs on the sides of the glass.

"So you didn't sleep with anyone else from the time you buried your pills in May until you slept with me in August?"

"Mostly no. Funny you, are you trying to clean me up in your fantasy?"

"And then what happened? You came to visit my mother."

"I came to visit your mother to invite her to dinner with Sally and me. And I rode my bicycle into Estérel instead of only calling because I thought I might walk around the town for an hour. I chained my bike up in the park and I walked to your apartment. On the way I bought some tiger lilies for you."

"For my mother."

"Yes, but I gave them to you."

"I remember them. They were striped and orange."

"That's why they call them tiger lilies. And then I bought a bottle of Merlot to drink with dinner. I had a basket on my bike, if you remember. And I rang your doorbell. For some reason I have a stronger memory of your apartment from that day than from any other. I could see it in my head before you opened the door. The door chimes in the front hall, the white painted wooden thingamabob from Mexico with the umbrellas in it and the framed print of van Gogh's *Arlésienne* over the striped couch in the living room."

She sips her wine. "You opened the door and I felt a little shock in my stomach. You stood behind the screen and I could see your pretty red mouth. Your hair was long; it covered your ears. There was something so fresh, and plump, and untrammeled about your face. Your neck was brown and smooth, and your T-shirt was thin and worn so I could see the circles of your nipples and your chest lifting and falling. You just looked so undefended, so gentle and innocent. You were perfect, untouched. And I wanted you. I wanted your breath in my mouth. I wanted your fingers inside me. I couldn't believe that the sweet, funny puppy that had followed me for years had grown into this golden hound. You were truly lovely."

Guy sniffs. He can feel himself blushing. "So you came in," he says.

"You opened the door and I walked in. I gave you the wine and flowers. In the kitchen while you were pouring the wine I took off my clothes. When you turned I kissed you and lifted your hands up to my breasts. I dragged you to the floor and undressed you. You were holding your hands in the air, surrendering. I took you in my mouth and I felt you shudder. I climbed onto your waist and you just stared at me. I had a moment of doubt and so I got off you. And then you came to me on all fours and fucked me on my back in the kitchen. So, the first time it took only a minute and you were contrite. But the second time it took three minutes, and the third time it took ten. By the time I left, we had drunk all the wine, sitting on the floor. We had yellow pollen all over our hands from the tiger lilies, and you and I had made love for an hour. If I hurt you it was because I didn't think I could. If I were the man and you the girl I would have known better. So I'm sorry. I'm sorry if I hurt you."

"Take me." Guy's voice comes out in an unchecked rush of sound. "Let's forget about Montréal and Ravel, and Boston even. Take me with you, somewhere."

"I can't."

He sips his wine and looks around at the other couples, quietly eating or speaking on the terrace. He feels embarrassed, realizing that they are still in public. The drumming overhead has ceased. The canvas awning begins to retract.

"'The gypsy knew in advance,'" he quotes softly, "'to tip up the barrels and spill out the night.'" Guy pauses to think. "'He slipped dimes through the lips of the poor with a kiss. This, he thought, is a starry map to hope.'"

"What is that from?"

"I can't remember. It's a poem from somewhere. It sounds like a good prayer."

They leave the green Alamo car in the parking lot of l'Hôtel d'Argenson. There is a wedding going on in the garden, so the little rental car is surrounded by black Cadillacs. The wind picks at white ribbons tied to dozens of antennae.

One follows the other through a rotating door into the mirrored lobby. The concierge is dressed in a red faux-military jacket with brocade on the shoulders. Harry approaches him as Isabelle falls to her knees to stroke a freckled spaniel swooning on the thick carpet before the desk.

Harry gently touches the marshmallow-shaped bell on the marble counter even though the man he wants already stands at attention.

"Can I help you, sir?" the concierge asks.

"Yes. We need a room for one night."

"What size bed, sir?"

"Large, king-sized. Is there anything bigger than king-sized?"

The man looks at Isabelle and studies her for a second. Her long hands fondle the black-almost-blue velvety ears of the spaniel. Her hair swings forward and covers her bare knees.

"No. Would you like two rooms?"

"No. One very large bed will be enough. I'll pay you in cash."

Alarm creases the man's neutral features. "Cash?"

"Yes, money."

"Um, yes, if you prefer, sir. We can take an imprint of your credit card and tear it up when you leave."

"But I don't have a credit card."

"Well." His eyes slide again to Isabelle. She meets his gaze with a glossy grin. He relents. "You can leave a cash deposit. Can you check your car keys until you leave?"

The room is almost perfectly square. There is a king-sized bed, a tiny window veiled by long, shimmering golden scrims, an armchair facing the bed, a mirror reflecting the armchair facing the bed, two matching night tables bearing two matching lamps, a Tuscan rose chenille spread folded back to show magenta sheets. Isabelle stands by the window, holding back the curtains.

"Isn't there an observatory in Ste-Famille?" she says finally. "Why have we never gone to the observatory?"

"I don't know. Turn on the light beside the bed, please," Harry says as he collapses into the armchair.

"Are you okay?"

"Yes. Can you see any stars?"

She nods. She reaches beneath the lampshade and turns the light on. The window becomes opaque.

"I saw the register. Jules and Jim are in room 12. Martine and Guy aren't here yet."

Isabelle sits on the bed and looks at herself in the mirror across the room. She looks skinny in the yellow lamplight. "They'll be here tonight," she says. "I'll set the alarm for five a.m. and then we'll wait outside the room for someone to come. Where is the washroom?"

"Down the hall, across from room 12."

"Why don't you come to bed? You have to sleep."

"I'm not tired yet. You can sleep, if you like."

Isabelle shrugs. She slips her sandals off and kicks them across the room. She undoes her skirt and lets it fall to the floor and then she kicks that too. After some contortions she manages to pull her bra out of the neck of her T-shirt. This she throws at Harry, who has been watching her undress with some amusement. He catches the bra and folds it, puts it beside him on the shelf below the mirror.

"Put your clothes away, Isabelle. Were you raised by wolves?"

"I was not raised by wolves and don't you nag me." She yawns and slides her legs under the covers.

"I'm going to the washroom to get ready for bed," Harry says.

When he returns, padding into the darkened room in cotton pajama bottoms, Isabelle is already asleep. The sheets are warm when he slips in beside her. He lies on his back, blinking at the darkness, sniffing the soft scent of Danish oil on the furniture, thinking of nothing but being unable to stop thinking altogether. Isabelle rolls over. Her breath grazes his shoulder. He wriggles away. A car horn bleats in the parking lot. He clears his throat and rubs his eyes.

Isabelle groans softly as Harry enters the bed after another trip to the washroom. He leans carefully up on his elbow and tries to unravel some of the sheets from around her body to cover himself.

"What are you doing?" she mutters.

"Go back to sleep. I'm just settling in."

"Why can't you sleep?"

He laughs shortly. "I'm thinking about tomorrow. I'm thinking about your mother. I'm worried."

"Don't worry."

"Okay, I won't worry." He settles in beside her with an agitated sigh.

"We're going to stop them from hurting Mom and Guy, don't worry. You know we can do it. We can save them. What's really the matter, Harry?"

"Where do you get your optimism from, Isabelle? Nothing else is wrong. I guess I just wish she could see me a little better. Then I wouldn't feel so stupid for worrying about her."

Isabelle sits up in the dark. "I can see you," she says. "I can see you."

She leans over him and her hair falls on his ticklish neck. He holds still, looking up at her face.

"Don't forget about me, Harry," she murmurs. "I know everything about you. I know that you don't like mustard, or bananas. I know that you sleep with an extra pillow when you're sick. I know all of your expressions and what they mean.

I know what you looked like when you were seventeen. I can see you. Please don't worry, Harry. Please don't be hurt. I know I have enough love for all of us."

Harry laughs and pushes her hair out of his face but he does not move away.

"The problem with you, Isabelle, is that you just don't worry enough."

"I worry. I just don't fret. It doesn't help to worry. It just burns up energy that you could use later to get yourself out of trouble."

"You're lucky to have that kind of control over your feelings. You know what? I think that it's our feelings that are the thing that's keeping us from living forever. If I could just stop worrying, if I could just stop my heart from getting warm or cold when your mother walks in or out of the room, I would be rich and I would die at two hundred without a line on my face."

"I don't think you would live very long at all."

"What's the point of all this feeling? I mean really, what makes feeling love a good thing? What makes it a survivable trait, when it makes us so reckless, and so nervous, and so sad?"

"Because love makes you brave. Do you want to know what I think? I think we need to fall in love to understand ourselves. Because being in love, it's just complicated enough and messy enough to be a good metaphor for being, and a motive to keep on being. I mean, it gives you a single place to put all the stupid questions that don't have any answers, like who am I, and why am I here? Love brushes all those things away. It does all kinds of other things, but the reason we keep on feeling it, and it doesn't go away, is because love makes you brave enough to face whatever it is you have to face."

"Yeah, well, that can sure work against you."

"Kiss me, Harry."

"What?"

"It's three o'clock. I'm scared too. I have feelings too. Don't talk anymore. Just kiss me. Why not kiss me? I love you, Harry. Don't even try to tell me I don't love you."

"Are you feeling sorry for me?"

"Yes. Please kiss me. Please."

She lifts his hand and kisses his palm. She lowers her mouth and kisses him. His lips are pliant, swelling under her mouth. She gives him weightless kisses. Gently feeling and tasting his lips, his teeth, touching his wet tongue with her own. She arches her back and presses her breasts against his lean chest. Her breasts flatten against her rib cage. The pressure makes her thin body feel strong. Harry neither fights nor assists her. He watches as she mounts his hips in shadow. She feels his erection rise against her damp underwear. He licks his lips, strokes her dainty waist and grips her hip. She slips a hand down and strokes her clitoris, moves her panties to the one side with a finger and opens his pajamas.

"I love you, Harry," she whispers. "I'm the one who loves you. Do I have your attention now?" She kisses him and whispers into his mouth, "I love you. I love you once. I love you twice. I love you more than beans and rice."

"Oh Jesus, Isabelle. Pretty baby," he laughs, uneasy, as his legs tremble. "How did I miss you? You're so good, Isabelle.

You're so crazy." He lifts his head as she bears down. "The world is so bad and you're so good." He opens his eyes and lifts his hands to cup her small soft breasts. He sees a flat spotty rash gather along her neck.

"It doesn't have to be a bad world," she says, bent knees clutching his sides. She leans over him, hands on either side of his head. "The most terrible things, Harry, they pass. Just fuck me, Harry. I promise, tomorrow everything will be different."

The television screen flashes in the still gray softness of the morning. Rob lies on the bed, dragging on a cigarette and sipping from a glass of orange juice. Axel poses with his gun, wearing just his jeans, unbuckled belt, his white feet, naked, dancing in the thick carpet. Onscreen, Madonna drives a silver car down a darkened street. She fondles a gun. Axel aims his gun at the lamp and pretends to fire repeatedly. Rob laughs at him. Axel whirls and swears and murders the shower curtain through the open bathroom door. Rob reaches for a croissant from a wire basket set on the night table. Axel thrusts his thin shoulders back and studies a vivid V of acne across his narrow chest. He scratches his chin with the muzzle of the gun and then throws himself onto the other double bed.

"Any time now," he says. "Bang, bang, bang, *bang*. Hand me a croissant."

Rob throws him a pastry. "Make sure we have the money first before you start acting out *Reservoir Dogs*, okay?"

"Mes bin sûr," Axel drawls in a grotesque accent.

Martine sits on the edge of the bed staring out at the apple orchards through the bay window. Black birds flurry up from the gnarled trees. The sun arcs through the calm sky. She looks back over her shoulder at Guy, naked, his slim body wrapped from the waist down in the white coverlet embroidered with silver thread.

"Don't sit up," she says. "I'm just going to talk to them. Stay in the room. If you wait for me more than an hour, it's too long. If that happens, take the car back to the train station and abandon it there. Call home and tell Isabelle to meet you at the train station. I brought a passport for her with me; you take it. Tell Isabelle and Harry to get away from the house as quickly as possible. I don't know if the police will go there or if Jules and Jim will come looking for them. Meet the kids at the station and take them to Boston. Leave a note for me with the ticket seller's booth. Or if there's an information booth, leave it there. Are you in the phone book?"

"Yes."

"Then you don't need to leave me a note at all. Just collect Isabelle and Harry and go home. Don't call me. Don't look for me. I'll find you as soon as I can."

Guy sits up and pulls his fingers through his hair. The hands on the little pentagonal alarm clock beside him lock into place and after a brief chirr the alarm begins to buzz insistently. Guy picks it up and turns a key in the back to choke the annoying noise.

"I want to come with you."

She shakes her head and pushes him back into the pillows. She reaches under the bed and grasps the shoebox.

There is a door to the washroom and shower stall in the narrow hallway outside room 12. The door bears a small metal frame with a Vacant/In Use sign that slides across when someone locks it from inside. Right now, the sign reads In Use. Isabelle stands behind the closed door. Harry stands outside the door, reading a newspaper, as if waiting patiently for the shower.

Isabelle leans her back on the door and studies the depressing stall beside the toilet and the pedestal sink. Square tiles are laid unevenly around a rusted drain. Water stains on the glass door resemble acid etchings. Isabelle sighs and crosses her arms on her chest.

Harry turns the pages of the newspaper at random. After a few minutes the door to room 12 opens and a young man exits. He glances at Harry and walks away down the hall. Harry knocks on the bathroom door. "We have the wrong room," he hisses.

"What?"

The Vacant sign slides into place. Isabelle sticks her head out.

"I just saw someone leave the room and he was my age."

"He must have been from room service."

"He wasn't wearing a uniform."

"Listen at the door."

Isabelle comes out and pulls the door shut silently behind her. The hallway is empty. As they step toward the room the electric lanterns along the walls become extinguished.

Engraved over the door, in the heavy, dark molding, is the number 12. Harry glances at his feet and sees how worn and gray the patterned carpet has become. Wood floors show through the ragged edges of the runners. He puts an ear against the door and holds his breath. From inside he hears a voice growling threats, "Hand me the money and close your fuckin' eyes," he hears someone say. "Don't look at me. You're already dead."

Harry swings his full weight on the door as he turns the handle. The lock is open and he falls into the room. A young man in the center of the room, the half-dressed, ugly man in the beautiful room, turns, startled. Harry sees that the man is alone, bare-chested in front of a mirror. The television is on and he recognizes the singer. The man raises his arm and Harry feels a sudden sensation like an arrow shooting through his forehead, he hears a cracking sound as his skull and scalp erupt with the bullet's exit, and then he feels heat escaping from his eyes. He hears Isabelle's voice screech as he has never heard it before and his

Blood from Harry's broken head is cast like ribbons across the floor. The edge of the throw rug soaks up the crimson load. Isabelle falls to the floor with him. She strokes his face desperately through the brief agonal heaving of his chest and shoulders. His mouth gapes, exhales a shrill whistle. The ugly man steps forward and aims his gun at her face. She raises her hands and pleads with him. He can barely understand her.

"Don't, don't, don't don't, don't," is what she tries to say.

The ugly man who bears the metallic stench of old sweat drags her by the arms and pushes her into a chair.

"Hang on. Hang on, Harry," she sobs.

"He can't," the man sneers. "He's got nothing to hang on to."

He shakes her by the shoulders. Her head falls back and forth. She sees him and he speaks again but she can't hear anything. She feels as if her insides are rent to pieces. Her lungs squeeze out air. Her ears fill as if from an abrupt descent. Her arms and legs are useless. The chair, the room, the bed, the window, Harry, the man and his gun are all caught up in a fog before her eyes. She vomits on the floor. The stench and the painful retching that follow leave her shaking and damp with sweat. The ugly man keeps talking.

"What's your name? What's your name?" he chants. "What are you doing here? What's your name? What's your name?"

"It was an accident. We have the wrong room," she whispers.

"What's your name?"

"Juliana."

"You don't look like a Juliana. If you were going to lie to me why didn't you go for something simple?"

Isabelle swallows warm bile and says, "My name is Kate. Who are you?"

"I'm Axel. Okay, Kate, do you want some water or anything?"

"No. I'm cold. Can I open the window?"

"No. Don't move."

He sits on the floor in front of her. His body blocks Harry from her view. She aches, in her head, her chest, her stomach. She stares at the silver-colored gun in his hand. He holds it casually between his knees. He looks so comfortable with a weapon it might be an extra digit extending from his palm. The muzzle gleams when he turns his wrist to check his watch.

"My friend should be back soon. Then we'll talk about you, Kate."

"I won't tell anyone you killed Harry. I won't tell anyone anything. Please. I'm only here on holiday."

He doesn't answer her. She can't bear to turn her head. She stares at the gun.

"You like my gun?"

"I like your gun," she stammers. "Can I hold it?"

"No."

"You can take the bullets out."

"It takes a cartridge. You're scared." He lowers his voice so that it almost sounds soothing. "I know you are. You're shaking and your throat and forehead are sweating." He touches her neck. "Can you even vote?"

"Why?"

"You look like a teenager. How old are you?"

Isabelle swallows. "I'm twenty. I can vote but my mother says that there's no point."

"Your mother said that?"

"Yes."

"She sounds crazy to me. Are you sure you don't want a glass of water? You must be pretty dehydrated by now."

Isabelle sniffs. She trembles so hard that her shoes clatter on the hardwood floor. She tries to say something else but her voice is strangled by tension in her throat. Finally, she manages to say, "Money-do-you-want?"

"Yes, Kate. Money. Of course that's what I want."

"Are you going to kill me?"

"Yeah. Yeah, I don't want to, but you know my name."

"You told me your name."

"Well, you asked."

"If I offered to have sex with you, would you let me live?"

He sighs. "I got to be honest with you, Kate. I can see you're cute. I would just kill you after I fucked you. Don't cry, Kate. Oh, come on. I'm going to shoot you through the roof of your mouth. It'll be fast. And the funeral director, he can sew the top of your head back on. You'll look fine."

"Please don't do that. I'll do anything. I'll . . . I don't know what you want."

"It's all right. I understand. I don't want to kill you. But, there it is."

"I won't remember you. I won't tell anybody you killed Harry. I won't, I won't. I promise."

"That's the stress talking. That's not true what you're saying. I don't enjoy killing pretty girls. I don't want to get your tears on my hands when I put my gun in your mouth."

She looks at the two beds, the open closet displaying a rack of shirts and suits. Beneath the bed, she sees an old brown suitcase on its side. A sticker, orange, pro-Trudeau, decorates the handle, probably to make the suitcase easier to identify rather than because its owner voted Liberal in the seventies.

"Where are they?" she says. "Are you friends of Jules and Jim?"

Axel leans into Isabelle's face. She blinks rapidly; her eyelashes graze his cheek. The gun is between her legs, pointed at the seat of the chair. Axel is crouched, leaning over her as if he might fall into her arms.

"Because," she tries, "we're friends of theirs too. We were only coming for a visit. We won't tell, I won't tell the police."

"Oh no. Oh no, Kate. I thought you said you were in the wrong room. I was only planning to frighten you. To fuck you, maybe, and then beat you unconscious. But if you lived, baby, I would have let that go. But now, no." He tsks. "It turns out you're the one I've been looking for. Where's the money? Let's get all the business out of the way."

"I don't have the money."

"I can't hear you. There's something wrong with your voice."

"I don't have the money. There's no money. That's what we were coming to tell them. We . . . I have some, but it's at my house."

"You're not making any sense. If I want a confusing story, I'll tell it myself. Your friend— He was your friend, right? He's dead, and I'm going to kill you too. But if you give up the money, I promise I'll do it really fast."

Isabelle feels his breath against her skin, each inhalation deepening after each exhalation. His body fills her point of view. The gun lies against her thigh, his knuckles rest there too, pinching her skin.

"I'll kill you so fast, it won't hurt. It will be a relief, after all this stress."

Isabelle lifts a hand to cover her mouth. The daylight shines red through her closed eyelids. She swallows and leans her cheek against Axel's cheek.

He is so startled that he pauses. She puts a hand down between her legs. With a start he seems to sense what she is doing and he fires the gun just as she pushes the muzzle under and away. A screaming hot pain rends his knee. His wrist twists and his full weight falls on his arm just as he understands that the shot has penetrated his leg. Isabelle pushes him to the floor and grabs the gun, which he releases to clutch his raw, opened joint.

"Holy fuck!" he screams. "You fucking bitch! I'm gonna rip your cunt out!"

She points the gun at him and touches the trigger. The door swings open and another man stands there. She wheels around and points the gun at the window, turns her face away and fires. The glass shatters with a sound like icicles falling onto a driveway. She drops the gun and runs to the window. At the window frame she stops. The fall to the ground is three stories. A wooden trellis covered in rose vines is beside the window. She steps out and grabs the vines. The thorns sink into her hands. She climbs out of the window and scrambles down toward the ground, ignoring the heat and pain as the thorns tear her palms and fingers, soles and toes.

Furious howls rise above her.

"Shoot her! Fuck, Rob, she shot me in my fucking knee! Shoot that cunt!"

"Shut up, Axel," she hears a stranger's voice say. Vicious expletives in response, a focused explosion and Axel's screams go silent.

The hotel rooms are empty but the halls are crowded. "Strange sounds," the guests are saying, "gunshots, two bodies." The concierge wears his uniform jacket over his dressing gown; he is trying desperately to assert himself over the panicked school of guests. His black spaniel follows at his heels, bumping into him and barking with excitement.

"Mesdames, messieurs, rentrez dans vos chambres. Nothing has happened, I assure you. Rien à faire! Nothing ever happens at l'Hôtel d'Argenson!"

"What happened?" Martine asks a stranger weaving down the stairwell.

The woman with long dark hair and small French features stands in front of Martine in a fragile camisole and cotton pajama bottoms, looking a little drunk.

"Two young people," she says. "I heard shots. Two young people are dead upstairs. I don't know if it was a murder or a suicide." Her voice flows on but Martine doesn't listen.

She fights her way through the hallways to the door of room 12. The door is ajar. Police have already covered the bodies with sheets stripped from the bed. The naked mattresses, Martine thinks, must be what makes everyone think that this is about love.

"Madame, ne touchez pas à la porte," a young policeman in a tight uniform addresses her gently.

"Qui est mort?" she asks.

The young man detects her accent and immediately switches to English.

"Are you a guest at the hotel?"

"Yes, I came in last night. I'm staying in room 4, downstairs. Who is dead? Is it a young man and woman?" she asks, her voice rising.

"Do you know who is here, staying in this room?"

"No. I'm not sure. My daughter and a young man, I'm afraid they may have followed me."

"Followed you? What do you mean?"

"I don't know," she cries. "Is it a man and woman dead? Can I see who it is?"

"It's two men, Madame. If you think you can identify them, I will close the door and show you."

He steps over one body as he strides to the doorway. The door makes a skeletal creaking as it closes. Another man emerges from the bathroom, also in uniform, also boyish. His hands are clad in latex gloves. He holds a Polaroid camera. He nods at Martine, and the two men make a brief exchange in what sounds like Spanish.

The first police officer crouches by the head of the nearest body.

"Vous êtes prête?"

"Oui."

He lifts the sheet gradually, allowing the bloody vision to unfold in increments. The face has no features. The skull is a dark and bloody chamber, lined with hair and bone. The neck is messy with matter. He is not wearing a shirt. Martine gasps for air.

"Do you know him?"

"No. No, thank God. I do not know him."

"I'll show you the other man now."

Martine nods. She feels the blood rushing back to her brain. She stands up and follows the young cop to the body by the door. She wraps her arms around herself and prepares to feel a wash of human pity. But when the sheet draws back, in fact before she sees a centimeter of skin, she knows. She watches the edge of the sheet as if it is a line separating the real world from the mad world. And when the line lifts she sees Harry, beautiful, ruined Harry.

"Do you know this man?"

There is a neat hole in Harry's temple edged with black. He has fallen backward and his hair obscures much of the worst damage at the back of his skull. His skin is pale, almost silvered. His face is flat and toneless. His eyes are open, pupils dilated, although it is obvious that they see nothing. The eyeballs look dry and slightly sunken. Martine has never seen a pair of eyes so still. She has never seen anything so utterly still.

"No," she says. "I don't know him either."

In the hallway she guards her steps, wary of her own instability. It is as if the air has become thick, too thick to move through. It takes tremendous energy to stand. She clutches at the door to the washroom, and when the crowd closes in the gap between her and the horrible room, she sobs. The door swings inward and she collapses on the tiles. She feels her legs being kicked out of the way and the door slams shut again. Suddenly another stranger is on his knees in front of her, his cheeks shaking, his teeth bared.

"Where's the money?" he hisses.

"Where's my daughter?" she says.

The guileless scent of strawberries rises from the ground beneath her faltering feet. She stumbles and runs, stumbles and runs. The blue-gray palisade of Mont Ste-Anne stands unaltered in the distance. She runs out of her shoes. Her skin is aflame with heat. It feels as though her heart is stretching. The strawberry leaves cannot protect her soles and toes from her own weight. At last she collapses, exposed on the horizontal plain. Her feet are stained with juice and blood. Her shirt is spattered with Harry's brains and blood. She pants and rolls on her back. The blue sky fills her eyes. She pants and rolls onto her knees. The fields stretch for miles. She looks behind her; the hotel is the only building, the only way. For miles, in every direction, there is nowhere to go.

Guy stands beside a window. The onlookers press him against the glass as they gradually remove themselves from the hallway. He has lost all track of Martine. It does not occur to him that the two dead men—victims, according to the susurrating crowd, of a murder-suicide—have anything to do with him. The sun turns the rippled window white. A cloud drifts into the sun's path and then he sees her. Or he sees something. Like a creature trying to outrun itself, she streaks into the solid green fields. He watches for a second, knowing that he sees something strange but unable to recognize the flailing woman. And then the scenery rearranges itself; he sees Isabelle collapse.

He takes her around the waist and leads her to the car. From a distance, the scene looks romantic. A couple is leaving a hotel hip to hip. He holds her flush against his side as if to squeeze the sunlight out from in between them.

The dust on the road whirls up around the tires and creates a tan contrail that follows the car. She looks out the window at a hawk perched on a highway lantern scanning the air for sparrows. The man leans his toes on the accelerator, feeling slightly ecstatic. The woman taps a cigarette out of a package and lights it with a red circle encased by a metal tube she draws from the dashboard.

She breathes smoke out of barely pursed lips. He glances over at her. Her legs are crossed tightly. He imagines her naked and then he feels thirsty.

"May I open my window?" she asks.

"No," he says. "Okay, just halfway."

They pass one apple orchard and then another. The short,

gnarled trees remind her of angry men, standing by the road, raising their arms in exasperation.

"Have you ever been to Switzerland?" she asks.

"I don't want to talk. And I don't want to listen."

"Can I turn on the radio?"

He checks the rearview mirror, shrugs his shoulders and pats the steering wheel, as if to encourage the vehicle. She leans forward and fiddles with the radio controls. The car is old; everything is on dials. An orange needle slides vertically along a set of white numbers indicating locations in the air. For minutes she finds only static and then a channel comes in, remarkably clear, playing French country songs, familiar to her from childhood.

"When we get to the house," she says, "I'll get you what you want and then I'd like you to leave me there."

"I was planning on leaving you there."

She leans her head back and draws on the cigarette. Sweat rolls down her neck into the neckline of her dress. She shifts her legs. She reaches into the pocket of her skirt and presses the hard, cold weight against her leg.

"I like," she says with calm surprise, "feeling helpless."

"Why?" he asks.

"I guess I like the feeling that it's too late. I like the idea that nothing I do, no action of mine, can possibly make any difference." She exhales smoke. "My daughter, Isabelle, was always like the seal around the door of an airplane for me. She was the piton in my hand; I hung on to her like I would fall to my death if I let go."

He looks at her but says nothing. He looks back at the road, but in his mind's eye he is still watching her hair, blowing across her forehead and over the headrest.

She quickly studies his face. He isn't any older than Harry. Smoke winds over her head as she exhales. She struggles to take a breath before asking, softly, "Did you kill my daughter?"

"No. She jumped out the window. She was trying to get away from my friend and me."

She nods. "I'm sorry about your friend."

"We weren't very close."

"It's funny. Now, I mean right now, here with you, I see my life getting shorter. But instead of having that Prufrock moment, which is what I expected, and feeling full of fear and counting up my mistakes, instead I find myself craving an inflatable raft and a large body of water. In my fantasy right now every second is taking longer to click into place, and I'm floating for a long, long time on a limitless ocean just waiting for the sun to rise and swallow me."

"I would like a holiday too," he says.

"I was wrong about some things. I argued that life was only a dream, I said it as if I meant that nothing matters. I forgot that the dream is the part of your mind that stays awake when all the rest is sleeping."

The tops of the pine trees blend together until it appears as if a black wire connects them. The radio loses the signal. A green sign over the highway indicates that they are approaching a turnoff.

"If you could take back one act, if you could wish one thing that you've done into oblivion, what would it be?" Martine asks.

"I don't know. Nothing, I guess. I don't regret anything I've done. What about you?" he counters.

"I think it will be the very next thing that I do."

Witnesses report that the young man's head seemed to lurch to the left as if struck by an invisible blow. His arm lolled out the open window and he did not straighten. The somnambulant vehicle sailed on for several meters, gaining speed before it struck the steel post of a highway sign on the east side of the road. The metal hood was crushed into the engine and the dashboard was crushed into the front seats. The deranged shape of the vehicle made it hard to see, at first, that a passenger lay hyperventilating inside. A litter of broken glass glittered on her shoulders. She did not answer the witnesses' calls. She gave a short series of great heaving breaths. A look of extreme languor crossed her face and all the tension left her body.

"Let me show you a trick," Isabelle says hoarsely.

She fishes in her purse. Back at the hotel Guy retrieved her things from her room while she waited, lying down in the backseat of Harry's car. He gave her the passport, which she opened and looked through slowly, as if she had not seen it before.

She takes a bill out of her wallet. A picture of Martine is engraved in the place of a president. Isabelle folds the bill twice and seals the folds between the nails of her thumb and forefinger. When she unfolds the bill, Guy sees two creases around Martine's mouth. Isabelle holds the bill at an angle tilted downward. The tilted creases make the image frown.

"I know this trick," Guy says. He takes the bill from her and tilts it upwards so that the edges of Martine's lips move into a smile. He turns his head and assesses Isabelle in profile. Her fine cheekbones are rouged from rubbing. Her neck and chest are scratched and bruised. Tears roll over her face and fall into her lap. She sips at an inch of scotch in a plastic tumbler and coughs.

"Martine will find us," he says.

She shakes her head. Outside the window the landscape spins backward. The trees, houses and fields fold into the past so quickly. At the next station stop, as the train slows, he watches a flock of Canada geese descend and begin sipping rain from puddles in the parking lot. Tension emanates from Isabelle's body braced in the seat beside him. He studies the two empty seats that mirror their own across a folding table lined with half a dozen empty miniature scotch bottles.

"How long until we get to Boston?" she asks.

Guy glances down at his wrist. "My watch stopped," he mumbles and shakes his wrist. The hands begin to check off time. "There it goes. It's working again."

At the train station Guy leaves Isabelle in a coffee shop while he uses the pay phone. He takes a piece of paper from his pocket, holds it up to the dial pad. The receiver feels warm against his ear. Three rings and then an answering machine clicks on. He hears a short drift of music and then a sharp tone.

"Martine," he says. "I know you probably aren't checking your messages but just in case you do, I wanted to let you know that Isabelle and I are having a lovely visit. I wanted to tell you that . . . I wanted to tell you that I'm glad I'm getting a chance to know her. But we both . . . Listen, if you want to reach us my address is 600 Atlantic Avenue. I'm in apartment 2. And my phone number is 617-973-3463. So you can reach me, if you want. Once again, it's 600 Atlantic Avenue, apartment 2, 617-973-3463. It's so loud here, I'm not sure if you can hear me: 600 Atlantic Avenue, apartment 2, 617-973-3463. I'm also in the phone book. Okay. All right, take care."

Acknowledgments

This book, like every book, was made possible by the assistance and support of many people. I want to try to thank all of them here. My thanks goes first to my editor, Patrick Crean, for his faith in me and for bringing me into the fold at Thomas Allen. Thanks also to the entire Thomas Allen team for good work and good natures. Thanks to my agent, Hilary McMahon, for many readings, much good advice and a cheery warm disposition. And to Nicole Winstanley, my former agent, Jennifer Barclay, and everyone else at Westwood who simultaneously guard me and present me to the world, thank you. Thanks to Gordon Robertson for the design of this book. I thank my family, Patricia and Russell Caple, Suzanne, Marc, and Paige Hicks, Gwyneth and Pip Probyn, Joyce Thomas and Eileen Caple for loving me even when I am not so lovable. I thank Christian Bök for being my consort over most of a decade. I thank Sandra and George Bök, Lori, Steve, Zane and Jett Isemann because I want to. I thank Nick Kazamia for being my only friend at 13 and my best friend at 33. I thank Kelly Ryan, David and Edna Magder, Jonathan Bennett, Wendy Morgan, André Alexis, Catherine Bush, Priscila Uppal, Chris Doda and Simon Archer for being good friends and models as I wrote this book. My thanks to Lynn Donohue for many honest discussions about sex. I thank Michelle Berry, Andrew Pyper, Russell Smith, Helen Tsiriotakis, Darren Wershler-Henry, Christian Bök, Hilary McMahon, and Gillian Fenwick for your intelligent readings and invaluable advice on this book at various stages; I thank Tatiana Freire-Lizama for medical advice (for Guy, not for me). Thank you Susan Swan for your mentorship and affection. Thank you Mali and Lesje for always being there when I wake up.